NURSE W

Dislike flares instantly between Nurse
Louise Weston and moody paediatrician
Mark Halliwell—until Louise is drawn
into the doctor's unhappy household and
begins to understand why he is so bad-
tempered. But to fall in love with him is
utter folly, surely, when she knows that
Mark is a man who can never be happy?

NURSE WESTON'S NEW JOB

BY
CLARE LAVENHAM

MILLS & BOON LIMITED
15–16 BROOK'S MEWS
LONDON W1A 1DR

CHAPTER ONE

'Is THERE a doctor on the train?'

The loud, important voice did not immediately penetrate Louise's absorption. She had been staring out of the window for some time, watching the countryside growing steadily more familiar. It was six months since she had seen it and winter had turned to radiant summer; even the salt marshes, which had begun to appear mistily in the distance, looked green instead of muddy brown.

As the stocky little man hurrying down the aisle repeated his question, she rose hastily from her seat.

'I'm a nurse. Can I help?'

Even at that moment he reacted at once to the sudden appearance of an attractive girl with shoulder-length, corn-coloured hair unusually teamed up with brown eyes. Her fair skin was evenly tanned and she looked cool and comfortable on a hot and sticky day in her sleeveless green summer dress.

'I reckon you could.' The man smiled appreciatively and halted in front of her. 'There's a bloke collapsed in the next carriage. Looks like it could be a heart attack.'

He began to retrace his steps and Louise followed him. On both sides passengers either stared after them with morbid curiosity, or displayed an urgent desire not to become involved by immersing themselves in their newspapers.

Although not a tall girl, she could see over her guide's shoulder and she did not need his pointing finger to locate her patient. An elderly man was lying across one of the tables, his arms outstretched, and all she could see at first was a mass of grey hair.

Bending over him she glimpsed greenish-white skin which glistened slightly, and when she touched it lightly with her finger it felt cold and damp.

'I think—' she began, and then glanced up in surprise as a peremptory voice spoke sharply from behind her.

'I should be obliged if you would get out of the way.'

A man of about thirty, wearing a well-cut, light grey suit, stood in the aisle. He had a lean, angular face and dark hair which gleamed with a slight reddish tinge in the sunlight. His black brows were long and elegantly shaped above eyes of a cold and unfriendly grey.

His tone had been even ruder than the actual words and Louise coloured with indignation. Nevertheless she controlled her temper and merely said quietly. 'I happen to be a nurse and I responded to a call for help.'

'I'm a doctor.'

He quite clearly considered that an adequate explanation for his abrupt manner and she immediately allowed him to take her place. His examination was brief and then he straightened up and delivered his verdict.

'It appears to be no more than an ordinary faint. The man will probably come round again quite soon, but in the meantime he should be lying flat.'

Well aware of that, Louise looked doubtfully at the narrow space available. 'There's not much room and people will want to pass up and down the train.'

'They'll have to step over him.' He looked round at the circle of watching faces. 'There's nothing whatsoever to stare at and I suggest it would be more helpful if you would all resume your seats instead of cutting off the air.'

Some of the spectators looked indignant, others a little ashamed, but they all did as they were told like obedient children and the doctor turned to Louise.

'I can manage his weight but you'd better—' He broke off as the passenger who had summoned assistance came bustling up with a plastic beaker in his hand.

'I got some water from the buffet car. I knew

you'd be sure to want to give the poor chap a drink.'

The doctor's face darkened. 'Good grief! You don't pour liquid down the throat of an unconscious man. Are you trying to kill him?'

Louise was not surprised to see the little man draw himself up angrily.

'There's no need to speak to me like that. I was only trying to help.'

'Well, you'll be of more use if you give me a hand here instead of the girl. She doesn't look strong enough to do much.'

Louise's lips tightened. Had he already forgotten she was a nurse and therefore accustomed to lifting?

'In that case,' she said curtly, 'I may as well go back to my seat. We shall be stopping at Deenham Market in a few minutes and I'm getting out there.'

She scarcely noticed that he had said, 'So am I,' for her eyes were on the man who had collapsed and she gave a sudden exclamation.

'I believe he's coming round.'

As she spoke the patient moved his head, bringing most of his face into view, and she leaned forward to get a better look.

'Goodness—it's William Taunton! He'll be getting out at Deenham too.'

'You know him?' the doctor asked.

'Oh yes, he's the local gardener and my

father is one of his employers. I didn't recognise him with his face hidden. Poor William—I wonder what made him pass out.'

'Probably the heat. It's very stuffy on this train and he's apparently used to an outdoor life.' He put a gentle hand on the man's shoulder. 'Take it easy. You'll soon feel better.'

Louise moved nearer and spoke in the soothing tone she used with anxious patients. 'It's all right, William. You've been feeling rather faint but I'm sure you'll be okay when you get out in the fresh air.'

'Miss Weston!' Faded blue eyes stared at her in astonishment. 'I thought you was abroad.'

'So I was, but I've come home now.'

'Whatever have I been doing then?' William glanced up at the tall young doctor. 'Fainting, you say? It never happened to me before—not in all my sixty-five years.'

'And it probably never will again,' he said with a friendly smile.

Louise averted her eyes from the phenomenon and took the beaker of water which had been so rudely refused a moment ago. 'I expect you'd like a drink now you're conscious again,' she suggested.

'Aye, I would.' He drank thirstily, grimacing at the taste, and she turned to the doctor.

'Please don't trouble yourself any more. I can cope quite well now and I'll see William safely out when the train stops.'

'Very well.' He gave her a long hard stare. 'I'll leave you to it.'

'Thank goodness he's gone!' the stocky little man exclaimed. 'I reckon he's one of those doctors who think they're God's gift to suffering humanity. Can't stand them myself.'

Louise couldn't either, but all she said was, 'He was nice to the patient and that's the important thing. Will you take charge for a moment while I fetch my suitcase?'

Five minutes later she escorted the elderly gardener to the platform and walked slowly beside him towards the exit. He was looking much better now, although his face had not regained its normal healthy colouring.

'I expect my father will meet me,' she said, searching for her ticket, 'and I'll ask him to give you a lift home.'

'That you won't, miss, thanking you kindly. I've got me bike at the station and I'll ride it same as usual.'

'Oh, William—I don't think you should! It's so hot.'

But he persisted in his resolution and she was obliged to give in. After all, he had only about a mile to ride and he would probably manage that all right.

'I was surprised to see you on the train,' she told him as they passed through the booking office. 'Have you been to Marchester?'

He nodded his grey head. 'I been to see my

little grand-daughter. You remember Kathy, the youngest of the bunch? She's been in the children's ward at the hospital there for a month or more. Got one of these new-fangled diseases with a long name I can't rightly recall.'

'Oh dear, I am sorry!' Louise exclaimed. 'Is she getting on okay?'

'Oh yes—she's coming home soon. There's a wonderful children's doctor, so they tell me, name of Halliwell, and he's done her a power of good. I haven't never seen him, meself.'

'I don't expect he comes round in the afternoon.' Louise halted against an ancient bicycle leaning against the fence. 'Is this yours?'

'That's right, miss.' William glanced round the station yard. 'Don't see no sign of your Dad.'

'I expect he'll be along in a minute.'

Louise had spoken confidently but, in actual fact, she was not so sure. The train had been at least fifteen minutes late and her father was notorious for impatience. In addition, he was a busy general practitioner and rarely had any time to waste. Maybe he had already turned up and then gone off again.

As she stood there beside her heavy suitcase, the ticket collector came hurrying out and accosted her.

'Oh there you are, Miss Weston. Your father left a message for you. Said he couldn't wait any longer and you was to take the taxi '

It had happened before and Louise wasn't altogether surprised. All the same, she couldn't help feeling it was rather hard to bear when she'd been away from home for so long. There was only one taxi at Deenham and it was more likely to be already booked. Certainly there was no sign of it in the yard now.

'I suppose I shall have to hang around and hope for the best,' she said resignedly.

'There's Fred now!' the ticket collector exclaimed. 'Just driving in.'

A one-time London taxi, which had clearly had a long, hard life, entered the yard at speed and raced to a stop near where they stood. But as Louise stepped into the road with relief, someone who had been waiting just inside the booking office also came forward.

'And about time too,' said a voice she had heard before. 'What kept you?'

Louise halted in dismay and at the same moment the taxi driver hailed her. 'Were you wanting me, Miss Weston? Oh dear, that's a pity. I'm booked to drive the doctor night and morning for two days because his car's laid up. What's happened to your Dad then?'

'He couldn't wait any longer. The train was late.'

'It certainly was, and a good thing too from my point of view, seeing as I was late as well.' He hesitated and looked over his shoulder at his passenger, who had already got in and was waiting in some annoyance for the conversation to end. 'I was wondering, sir, if you'd mind if we gave Miss Weston a lift? It wouldn't take you out of your way no more than a quarter of a mile or so.'

There was a horrible pause. Louise was just beginning to say hurriedly, 'It doesn't matter in the slightest. I'll wait until you come back, or perhaps my father will turn up after all—' when the young doctor she had so much disliked on the train interrupted her.

'Very well, since there seems to be only one taxi.'

'It's extremely kind of you,' Louise forced herself to say.

'Not at all.'

Fred took her suitcase from her and she got in, sitting down as far as possible from the other occupant. As they began to move she stared out of the window, her shoulder slightly hunched.

'That man who collapsed,' he said abruptly. 'Didn't I see him riding off on a bicycle?'

'Yes. He insisted.'

'I believe you said you were a nurse. Do you usually allow your patients to decide for themselves what's good for them?'

Louise turned round indignantly. 'Of course not, when I really *am* in charge, but this was different. William Taunton had a perfect right to make up his own mind.'

'That's a matter of opinion.'

'Oh yes,' she agreed, 'and that means I'm entitled to mine, just as you are to yours. I suppose you think I should have consulted you before I let the old chap ride away?'

'I would at least have attempted to dissuade him,' he said stiffly.

To her annoyance she found herself offering an explanation of her attitude, which was almost an apology. 'I'm afraid I've got used to deciding things for myself recently. I'm a private nurse and I've been looking after a patient who lived in Corsica. It was a chronic case and the local doctor left me very much on my own.'

'What happened to your patient?'

'She—er—died.'

Louise had expected him to say 'There you are then!' with an air of triumph, but instead he made a totally different comment. His eyes, no longer cold, were on her bare, tanned arms and sun-kissed face.

'No wonder you look as though you've been on holiday. I should think it hardly seemed like work at all.'

'It did at times! My patient was a difficult type—wealthy and used to bossing people around. She gave me quite a lot of trouble.'

'No doubt you were well paid for it.' His voice, which had become coolly friendly, changed again. 'I imagine that's why nurses give up hospital jobs and take these private cases. The salary is so much higher.'

'I didn't do it for that,' Louise told him indignantly. 'For your information, I worked for four years at Marchester General and then I decided I wanted to travel. I've had half-a-dozen cases around the Mediterranean area and enjoyed most of them very much.'

'I don't suppose you'll ever want to return to hospital nursing. It wouldn't be glamorous enough for you.'

She bit back a sharp reply. Couldn't the man distinguish between a natural desire to visit foreign places, and what he called 'glamour'? No doubt he wouldn't believe her if she told him she quite often missed hospital life and the company of other nurses, that she was actually thinking of going back to it now that she no longer had itchy feet.

They lapsed into silence, both of them staring out at the flat green fields of young corn or sugar beet, the occasional cottage and every now and then those glimpses of the marshes.

'Where do you live?' the doctor asked suddenly.

'Holly Lodge, Barkington. We shall be there in a minute.' On an impulse, she added, 'My father is the local GP, which is why he couldn't wait for me. He works on his own and is kept very busy.'

He made no comment, and at that moment

Fred began to slow down. He pulled up outside a wide entrance from which the gate had long ago disappeared. A large holly tree partially hid the house, but Louise could see the front door standing open and a surge of excitement seized her. It would be wonderful to be home again.

'There you are, Miss Weston.' Fred jumped out with her case as she flung a hasty word of thanks towards the silent young man in the car. 'I'll just carry this up the drive for you.'

'No, please don't bother,' Louise said hastily. 'Your passenger has been delayed enough already.' She almost snatched the case from him.

He hesitated and then evidently decided she meant it. 'Okay then,' he agreed cheerfully. 'Glad we were able to help out.' Already climbing back into his seat, he called over his shoulder, 'You'll soon be home now, Dr Halliwell.'

Halliwell! Momentarily diverted from the coming reunion with her mother, Louise stared after the departing vehicle. Where had she heard that name recently? Why, of course, William had mentioned it. Dr Halliwell was the paediatrician who had done so much for his granddaughter.

It was almost beyond belief that such an extremely dislikeable sort of person was a children's doctor. She just couldn't imagine him in the informal and often chaotic surroundings of a children's ward in a big hospital. With a shrug she dismissed the matter and began to walk quickly up the drive.

The garden testified to William Taunton's skill. On the right a big bed of Queen Elizabeth roses lifted their proud pink heads to the sun, and beyond it Louise could see a stretch of lawn and a long herbaceous border glowing with colour. And half-way along it, someone in a blue dress and a big sunhat cutting flowers for the house.

'Hi, Mum!' She put down her case, jumped over a low box hedge and ran across the grass.

Marion Weston turned with an exclamation of surprise. 'I didn't hear your father's car. How are you, dear? It's lovely to see you.'

Louise explained what had happened, making it sound amusing when, in fact, it hadn't been like that at all. And although Marion was clearly annoyed with her husband, she accepted it as the sort of thing he was likely to do.

'What was your impression of Dr Halliwell?' she asked curiously. 'We haven't met him yet as he's only been here a few weeks. He bought that house overlooking the marshes which has been empty for some time.'

'Creek House? What a lonely, isolated sort of place for a young man—though, on second thoughts, I can't help thinking it would suit his personality.'

'It sounds as though you didn't take to him.'

'I wasn't impressed. Is he married?'

'He *has* been but I'm not sure about the present situation. You know how country people talk about new arrivals, specially if they don't mix. There's a child, by the way, a little girl who's just started coming to the play school in the village.' Marion put a final flower into her basket and began to walk towards the house with Louise at her side.

'The man doesn't really have any time for socialising,' she went on. 'I can't think why he chooses to live fifteen miles from his job and it must be very inconvenient when he's called out for emergencies. However, that's his worry and nothing to do with me. Where's your luggage, dear?'

'In the middle of the drive.' Louise laughed and went to fetch it.

The house was shadowy and cool, with drawn curtains keeping out the heat of the sun. Marion went round pulling them back to let in the early evening breeze, and Louise took a quick shower. Downstairs again, with a long cool drink in her hand, she leaned back in her chair and gazed dreamily out through the open french windows.

It was nice to be home, lovely to think that four weeks of summer holiday stretched ahead of her, weeks in which she needn't answer any imperious bells rung sometimes for no reason at all—or, in fact, do anything she didn't want to. Four whole weeks of glorious laziness.

She couldn't have been more wrong.

CHAPTER TWO

FOR THE first two weeks everything was exactly as Louise had imagined it. The good weather continued and she lazed in the garden, swam in a neighbour's pool and went for long walks on the marshes. She had known them since childhood and was well aware of the danger due to the speed at which the numerous creeks could fill when the tide came in.

Once or twice she passed Creek House, but she saw no sign of life. It stood at the end of a narrow, straight road bordered by dykes, turning its back on the village and looking towards the distant sea. The garden stretched down to the banks of a wide creek which always contained water, whatever the state of the tide.

It was a wild, lonely place with—so Louise thought—something slightly sinister about it. Much as she loved the marshes, she wouldn't have liked to live there herself.

At the end of her second week the weather changed. Grey clouds hid the sun and tennis seemed more attractive than swimming. There was a shabby old court at Holly Lodge and Louise set herself the task of making it usable. She cut the grass and dragged out an ancient roller with a view to getting rid of the bumps.

She was dragging it behind her, gasping and uncomfortably aware of scarlet cheeks, when a curt voice addressed her suddenly from the drive.

'Are you deliberately trying to give yourself a slipped disc?'

Her retort was instinctive, leaving her lips almost before she realised that she recognised the voice.

'I'm not that daft!'

'But daft enough to try and pull something which is obviously much too heavy for you.'

Dr Halliwell stood there, his angular face as unsmiling as she remembered it, his whole attitude indicative of male superiority, and Louise reacted fiercely.

'It's my own business if I choose to roll the tennis lawn, and this roller is *not* too heavy for me. It's only difficult to move because it's hardly ever used.'

'Did you say tennis lawn?' he asked incredulously.

'Yes, I did!' Her flushed face burned even more hotly. 'I'm trying to make it fit for use, which I should have thought was perfectly clear, so perhaps you'll go away and leave me to get on with it.'

But instead of doing that he stepped over the box hedge and walked towards her, his long strides rapidly reducing the distance between them. Louise watched his approach with dismay. She couldn't imagine what he wanted, and the nearer he came the more her apprehension grew, though she could think of no reason why she should feel like that.

'I want to talk to you,' he said abruptly. 'Can we sit down?'

Louise looked up at him in astonishment, but he was staring over the top of her head towards a white-painted seat which over-looked the tennis court.

'I suppose so.' She led the way to it reluc-tantly, totally averse to spending any more time with this man whom she so much disliked. Her cardigan was lying on the back and she paused to slip her arms into it. 'What on earth do you want?'

'Your professional help.'

'But—but I'm on holiday. I told you.'

'You've had two weeks and can't be in actual need of any more. Besides, I shan't interrupt your vacation for more than a day or two.'

Louise's bewilderment increased. 'I wish you'd explain—'

'I'm about to do so.' He leaned back, stretching out his long legs, but though the attitude was relaxed she could see that the tenseness had not left his hands. There was a tautness about the way his long brown fingers were intertwined that told a different story. He was clearly uptight about something and, as she waited, Louise began to feel strangely nervous.

'I have a small daughter, Vicky, aged four, who is at present ill in bed. She normally attends a play school and she seems to have picked up some bug. I don't think it's serious but she needs nursing care for a short time. It occurred to me that you might be willing to take the case.'

'*Me*?' She did not try to conceal her amazement. 'Can't you get an agency nurse?'

'You, I believe, are an agency nurse, and the matter is urgent.'

'But who usually looks after Vicky? Surely you have someone to run the house?'

'I was coming to that. My housekeeper, unfortunately, has chosen this particular time to fall downstairs and break her ankle. She is at present in the hospital in Marchester and, though I don't suppose she will be kept in for more than a day or so, I need someone now.'

There was no sympathy for the poor woman in his voice, Louise noted indignantly. He plainly felt she had deliberately slipped on the stairs in order to make everything as difficult for him as possible.

She said diffidently, 'Wouldn't it be a better solution to take your little girl to Marchester too? You're the paediatrician in charge of the children's ward, aren't you? Surely you could find a bed for her and she would get the best possible attention there.'

'No doubt she would,' he retorted indignantly. 'But I shouldn't dream of taking advantage of my position to thrust my own child into the ward when she doesn't require hospitalisation. Vicky can perfectly well be nursed at home.'

'Provided you can find someone to do it.'

'Exactly.'

'And I suppose you think you have?'

'I'm certainly hoping you won't refuse.'

Until that moment Louise had had every intention of doing just that. Why should her holiday be spoilt just because she happened to live near Creek House? He could quite easily have got some other nurse to take it on.

But could he? The nearest agency was probably in London and, as he had said, he needed someone now. Louise's imagination instantly painted a pathetic picture of a small, forlorn girl in a tumbled bed, crying her heart out because there was nobody to give her the tender loving care she so badly wanted.

Would she ever forgive herself if she didn't help?

'All right,' she said resignedly. 'I'll do it. I suppose you want me to start this very minute? I'd better go and get ready.'

She had not really expected fulsome thanks

and she got no more than a brief, 'Okay then. I'll wait for you in the car.'

In the house her mother listened in astonishment to her story, agreed that it would have been difficult to refuse, and left her alone to pack the few things she required.

'I didn't bring my uniform,' she said when she rejoined the doctor. 'I didn't think your little girl would like it.'

'It's up to you.' He started the engine of a red, sporty-looking car and drove rapidly down the road leading towards the marshes.

The short drive to Creek House was accomplished in silence. As they approached it Louise thought yet again what a gloomy place it was on a grey morning. It was built of dark red brick and had a slate roof, and even the garden seemed lacking in colour for July.

Not that it mattered very much. She wouldn't be there long enough to mind either the isolation or the dreariness.

'I'll take you straight up and then I must leave for Marchester. I'm very late as it is.' Dr Halliwell passed swiftly through a square hall with black-and-white tiles, where dead flowers drooped on the table, and ran up a steep, straight flight of stairs. As Louise followed she found herself thinking that the unknown housekeeper had been lucky not to break her neck.

On the landing he paused. 'I'm afraid I haven't a clue what your name is.'

'Louise Weston.'

'I'm Mark Halliwell. You won't mind if I introduce you by your christian name? I don't suppose Vicky will want to call you Nurse.'

Assuring him that she would prefer it, Louise scurried after him down a passage leading towards the back of the house. He flung open a door and strode into a large, untidy bedroom where toys spilled out of cupboards and bowls and plates containing half-eaten meals were scattered around. In the middle of the chaos was the tumbled bed of her imagination; a small, fair head lay on the pillow and large greenish eyes regarded them with a frightened stare.

'I've brought someone to take care of you, Vicky,' Mark Halliwell announced in a businesslike tone. 'Her name is—er—Louise.'

There was no answer. He frowned and put his fingers on the thin little wrist. Louise directed a friendly smile at this unexpected patient and awaited her instructions.

'She must stay in bed, of course, and it doesn't matter if she eats very little. It's far more important that she should have plenty of fluids.' He looked down at his little daughter and patted her head with a slightly awkward gesture. 'I must go now, Vicky. Try and be a good girl and do as Louise tells you.'

As the door closed behind him and she was left with a stranger, the child buried her face in the pillow with a sob. Collecting the dirty plates, Louise talked quietly about nothing very much, doing her best to establish a link with the forlorn little creature so surprisingly given into her care.

It was some time before she got any response and then Vicky suddenly raised her head and gave her another apprehensive stare.

'I s'pose you're a new Anna.'

Louise paused in bewilderment. Had the little girl intended to say 'nanna'? Perhaps she was referring to a grandmother. It was the popular name for elderly female relatives these days. And yet she was old enough to realise that Louise didn't qualify in any way for such a title.

'Did you say nanna?' she asked cautiously.

'No, of course not. I said Anna.' And she added helpfully, 'She fell downstairs and broke her ankle.'

'Oh, you mean the housekeeper! No, I'm not taking her place—at least, not in that way. I'm only here to look after you.'

Vicky's eyes filled with tears. 'I don't know you. I want Anna.'

It took all Louise's patience and genuine sympathy for the little girl to coax her into a happier frame of mind. She had plenty of experience in nursing children, with a long

spell on the children's ward during her training, and gradually she began to feel she was
making contact. As she tidied the room,
washed her patient and changed the bedlinen,
time began to fly past and suddenly she realised she was starving.

She stayed with her patient until Vicky fell
asleep and then explored the kitchen. It was
not an encouraging sight, with the draining
board piled with dirty dishes and several used
saucepans in the sink.

There didn't seem to be much food, except
in the freezer, which was well stocked but
wildly untidy. She found a tin of chicken soup
and some bread and cheese and fruit, and
carried her frugal meal outside, leaving the
doors open so she would hear if Vicky woke
up.

As she sat on the terrace it occurred to her
that she had done nothing about preparing a
bed for herself. If only her employer hadn't
been a doctor, working unsocial hours, she
could have gone home each night, but under
the circumstances it wasn't practicable. She
had no idea when he might return but guessed
it might be pretty late, since he had started his
day so much in arrears.

Upstairs again, she peeped into several
rooms, looking for one for herself. The big
front room on the left of the porch was
obviously Dr Halliwell's, though he appeared

to have done little to stamp his personality on it. It was almost clinically tidy. The other, similar room must belong to the housekeeper, since it was definitely feminine with an array of bottles on the dressing-table and clothes carelessly flung down.

There was a connecting door between the two rooms, to which—at the time—she paid little attention.

Apart from Vicky's there was only one other furnished room on that floor. It was dusty and disused, but Louise found sheets and blankets and made up the bed. As she did so she thought wistfully of her attractive room at Holly Lodge and wished more fervently than ever that she needn't stay the night.

Mark Halliwell did not come home until half-past ten and Louise, bored and lonely, was again outside, gazing dreamily out over the marshes where the last traces of orange still lingered in the sky. It was so still she could hear the soft wash of the sea, and suddenly a new sound was superimposed—the purr of a fast car.

Headlights swept up the short drive, flinging trees and bushes into relief, and Louise abandoned her solitary vigil and walked round the house into the blaze of light.

'Everything okay?' The doctor got out and stretched wearily. 'I hope Vicky's behaved herself.'

'She's been very good,' Louise answered
him curtly, annoyed that he had asked about
the child's behaviour and not how she was
feeling. She went on to give details of temperature and pulse rate, though she sensed he was
paying little attention.

His head was inside the car and he was
collecting parcels from the back seat, eventually emerging with his arms full.

'I don't know if you found anything to eat,
but I shouldn't think there was very much.'

'Soup and bread and cheese. Everything
else was frozen.'

'As I thought, so I called in at the Chinese
take-away before I left Marchester and
brought enough for us both. Come on, let's go
inside.'

He led the way into the house and through it
to the kitchen, where he spread the table with
a red-and-white gingham cloth and dumped a
handful of knives, forks and spoons on it.

'Sort them out, please, while I see to the
food.'

Not really believing in any of it, Louise did
as she was told. When a bottle of red wine was
produced, and two glasses, she was ordered to
search in a drawer for a corkscrew and meekly
did so, even experiencing a sense of triumph
when she found it.

'You can have white if you'd rather,' Mark
said, 'but it won't be chilled.'

'I'll have the red, thank you.'

For a while he ate hungrily without speaking and Louise did the same, finding that the frugal meal she had consumed earlier had made little difference to her appetite. After a while the silence began to worry her and she asked if he had seen his housekeeper that day.

'I called in before I left. She'll be allowed home tomorrow, thank goodness, but—er—I'm afraid she won't be able to manage the stairs for a bit.' He came to an abrupt halt, his eyes on Louise's face.

The wine was making her feel pleasantly relaxed and his full meaning did not immediately sink in. When it did, she sat up with a jerk.

'What about Vicky then? She isn't fit to get up yet.'

'Definitely not. So I hope you'll agree to remain a little longer?'

Louise stared back at him indignantly. 'You said it would only be for a couple of days, and now you're asking me to remain indefinitely.'

'Only until Vicky can get up.'

'But you must have known the housekeeper wouldn't be able to manage those terribly steep stairs. I consider you've got me here under false pretences.'

'You're exaggerating,' he said coldly. 'And, anyway, since you're supposed to be a nurse you should have been able to work out for yourself that Anna would find the stairs impossible.'

'How dare you talk to me like that!' Louise jumped to her feet. 'Supposed to be a nurse indeed! Don't you remember I told you I was trained at your hospital? I was a staff nurse there before I became an agency nurse and I've had a great deal of experience.'

Mark had not risen. Instead he leaned forward with his arms folded on the table and regarded her angry face with interest.

'You should lose your temper more often. It suits you.'

For a moment she was speechless, and then she burst out furiously, 'You should be a good judge of people losing their tempers. I should think you're frequently the cause of it.'

To her gratification he looked slightly taken aback. 'I hadn't noticed, and I don't think I know what you mean.'

'I mean that you have a gift for annoying people. I noticed it the moment we met on the train.'

'Really?' His dark, elegant brows rose so high they almost touched the thick hair cut straight across. 'You're the first person who's ever mentioned it and, personally, I think you have a vivid imagination. Shall we wash up and then make some coffee?'

Biting her lip, Louise went to the sink and turned on the hot tap. He really was an absolutely impossible man and she couldn't even have contemplated staying on in his house if she hadn't known that most of his time would be spent in Marchester.

And yet, when the chores were done and they carried their coffee into a small, untidy room which he referred to as the study, his mood changed completely. Making conversation, Louise had asked him whether he really liked the lonely position of his house.

'Don't you find the marshes a bit depressing sometimes?' she suggested. Her question seemed to surprise him and he answered emphatically.

'Never. After the noise and fumes of Marchester they seem a haven of peace and quiet. There are times when I infinitely prefer the cries of sea birds to the sound of human voices, particularly when the voices have been saying things which are more than usually foolish.'

'You think people often talk foolishly?'

'In my experience they do.'

'I'm afraid you must have been unlucky. I've always loved the marshes but I've rarely wanted to escape there to get away from people. Once or twice when I was a teenager, perhaps, and my brothers or my boyfriend had annoyed me, but not since.'

'You belong to a big family?' he asked politely.

'Oh no, there are only four of us and I'm the youngest. The others are all married.'

'Four seems a lot to me. I find Vicky quite enough of a problem.'

Louise would have liked to follow up that opening but could think of nothing to say that wouldn't sound critical of his role as a father. Instead, she asked if he didn't find living at Barkington inconvenient when he was summoned to the hospital in an emergency.

'Not in the least. What's fifteen miles in a fast car, particularly at night? I can reach the ward almost as quickly as though my house was on the outskirts of Marchester.'

He had a point there, she supposed, and at that moment there was an outburst of crying upstairs.

'Won't you come and say good-night?' she asked at the door.

Mark shook his head. 'Vicky doesn't expect it. It's better for you to go to her by yourself.'

As she attended to the little girl's needs, Louise was puzzled. It never seemed to occur to the doctor that his child might require more from him than attention to her physical welfare.

She did not see him again that night, and in the morning he left for Marchester before she rose—a little late after being disturbed several times by her small patient. Vicky seemed worse today but Louise was not seriously concerned about it, knowing that the germ must take its course for a while.

She was so busy that she completely forgot that the housekeeper was due to return some time during the day.

The sudden appearance of an ambulance outside the house reminded her at once and she went downstairs to see if any help was required.

One glance was sufficient to show her she wasn't needed. Two ambulance men were walking slowly on either side of their patient, talking, laughing and assisting her with exaggerated care as she struggled along on crutches.

But this wasn't the middle-aged housekeeper Louise had been imagining. Anna was young—probably about her own age—and she had long, silky gold hair and eyes as blue as sapphires. Her face was not classically beautiful but it glowed with health and vitality in spite of her unfortunate experience.

As she went forward to greet her, Louise suddenly remembered the connecting door between the two front rooms and everything seemed suddenly to fall into place.

CHAPTER THREE

WHEN LOUISE appeared on the top step Anna looked up and her eyes widened.

'Who can you be? Has Mark obtained a temporary housekeeper?'

Although her English was fluent, if a little too precise, she had a definitely foreign accent and Louise guessed that she was probably Danish. Uncomfortably aware that antagonism had leapt like a spark between them, she hastened to explain her presence.

'I'm the nurse looking after Vicky. Didn't Dr Halliwell tell you he'd asked me to help out?'

'Yes indeed, but you don't look like a nurse. I thought you would wear uniform.'

'It seemed better to keep to ordinary clothes,' Louise explained briefly. She watched as the ambulance men supported their patient up the steps. 'I've made you up a bed in the dining-room,' she went on, retreating into the hall. 'Dr Halliwell said it's never used for meals.'

Anna wrinkled her shapely nose in disgust. 'I shall not enjoy sleeping in that dark, dreary room, but certainly the stairs will be too much for me at first.' She gave a sudden exclamation. 'I have not asked after my little Vicky. She is better?'

'Not yet—she seems to have picked up a particularly unpleasant virus—but I think there'll be some improvement by tomorrow.'

'I must see her. She will have missed me most terribly.' Anna lowered herself carefully onto the hall chair. 'You will bring her to me, please.'

It was definitely an order and Louise reacted instinctively. 'She isn't well enough to come downstairs.'

'You can carry her. If she is wrapped warmly it will do no harm to her body and I think it will make her mind much happier—yes?'

Aware that this was true, Louise gave in. Upstairs she found Vicky already sitting up in bed and calling out eagerly.

'Anna—I want Anna!'

'She can't come up to see you until her ankle is better, love, but I'll take you down to say hello.'

She descended the perilous stairs carefully with her burden and handed the child over to the housekeeper, who received her with exclamations and a warm embrace. There was no doubt at all about the affection between the two.

There were tears when Vicky had to be returned to bed and Anna clicked her tongue disapprovingly. The incident marked the start of a long, difficult sort of day. Louise tried to be as helpful as possible and yet not to let herself be put upon. The Danish girl, clearly, did not understand the special position which a trained nurse holds in a private household; she was much too inclined to give orders and expect obedience.

Mark was home early. He came into the kitchen where Anna was preparing vegetables and Louise doing the fetching and carrying, and for the first time Louise saw him smile with real warmth.

'It's great to see you back, Anna! How are you feeling?'

'I am not too bad. Somehow we manage.'

He sat down at the kitchen table and continued talking while Louise went on silently with her work. He hadn't even asked after his small daughter, she thought resentfully, and seized the first opportunity to mention her.

'Vicky seems a little better this evening. I think she's turned the corner now.'

'So she should, with all the antibiotics I've been giving her.' Mark stood up. 'Perhaps I'd better take a look.'

As soon as the door closed behind him Louise exploded. 'You'd never think he was the child's father! He doesn't seem to take any real interest in her at all.'

Anna did not immediately reply. She

finished slicing a carrot neatly and then shrugged. 'To me it seems that Mark is not what you would call a family man.'

'And yet he's a paediatrician. He must be interested in children or he wouldn't have chosen that branch of medicine.'

'I think he chose it earlier—before Vicky was born.'

'And what's that supposed to mean?' Louise demanded indignantly.

'His marriage was not a happy one and the birth of a child did not mean as much to him as it would have done under other circumstances.'

Anna's tone had been evasive and Louise was puzzled. 'He's divorced, then?'

'Oh no. Vicky's mother died when she was born.'

'So she's never had a real mother, poor little thing. That might explain why she seems so forlorn.'

For some reason Anna seemed offended. 'Vicky is not forlorn when she is well. As soon as she is better and can get up and come downstairs again, you will see the difference.'

'But I shan't be here then!' Louise exclaimed. 'Dr Halliwell only asked me to come for a couple of days and today is the second one. I really ought to be leaving tomorrow.'

'Tomorrow? Most certainly you cannot. How can I manage with Vicky still in bed and no one to help me?' Anna twisted round on her chair as the door opened. 'Mark, you must explain to the nurse that she can't possibly go until the child is quite well. Even then it will be difficult for me—'

'Is Louise talking of leaving?' he asked in surprise. 'I thought everything was working out rather well.'

'The agreement was only to last a very short time,' she reminded him, making no attempt to keep the exasperation out of her voice. 'Perhaps you've forgotten I'm in the middle of my holiday?'

'You can easily make the time up later—add another week or something. An agency nurse pleases herself, doesn't she? I really do think you must agree to remain here at least until next week.'

Louise's brown eyes flashed dangerously. 'There's no *must* about it.'

'I'm sorry.' It sounded as though the apology nearly choked him. 'Let me put it differently. We really need your help here and therefore I hope very much that you will stay a little longer. I'm afraid I was so thankful to get you to Creek House that I didn't look very far ahead, but you can see for yourself that Anna won't be able to do very much.'

It was perfectly plain to Louise that he was right, though she still felt she had been led up the garden path. Since the only reason she had for insisting on leaving was the fact that she wanted to go rather badly, she was obliged reluctantly to conclude that she must give in.

'Very well,' she said curtly, 'I'll nurse Vicky until she's fit again, on the condition that you get someone in from the village to do the housework. I don't mind helping with the cooking and I'll keep Vicky's room clean, but I draw the line at taking on all the other domestic chores.'

'Housework is not important.' Anna was looking stubborn. 'So long as we eat well—'

'*You* may be used to living in a pigsty,' Louise flashed, 'but I'm not!'

'For goodness' sake—' Mark was at the end of his patience and his explosion came just in time to stop an angry outburst from Anna. 'I never heard such a hell of a fuss over something so trivial! But certainly I'll find a cleaning woman to help out if one can be obtained.' His finely-marked brows drew together in a worried frown. 'Unfortunately I haven't a clue how to set about it.'

Louise hesitated. All her instincts were telling her not to get any more involved than she was already, and yet it seemed unnecessarily unhelpful not to mention the idea which had come to her.

'You remember William Taunton, the man who fainted on the train?' she said to Mark. 'His wife does cleaning. I think she would come here temporarily if—if I asked her.'

'That is good!' Anna exclaimed. 'You will ask her at once, Louise. She lives near Creek House?'

'There are no houses really near, and I don't think Mrs Taunton would want to walk down that long, straight road from the village. She would need transport.' Louise looked pointedly at Mark. 'You would have to fetch her before you went to Marchester.'

'I suppose I could manage it, provided I hadn't been sent for in a hurry. You'd better go and see the woman this evening after dinner.' Belatedly he added, 'I'll drive you.'

'Thanks, but I'd prefer to walk. I've been indoors all day,' she said firmly, and he did not try to dissuade her.

Perhaps he wanted to be alone with Anna?

It was still daylight when she set out, glad to be away from the house and in the fresh air. It was particularly fresh this evening, blowing damply across the marshes, where the numerous little creeks were rapidly filling as the tide came in, and ruffling Louise's hair as she walked swiftly down the road.

The Tauntons lived in a semi-detached cottage made of local flint, and with a neat front garden in which potatoes flourished next to a mixed border of summer flowers. William and his wife were surprised and pleased to see Louise and Mrs Taunton at once agreed to help at Creek House.

'But I wouldn't want to go there regularly,' she said flatly. 'Gloomy old place, to my mind. I can't think why the doctor chose to live there, not that what he does is any of my business, though you can't help hearing things when you live in a village. Anyway, I'm glad to be of assistance to a man who did so much for our Kathy.'

'She's fit again now?'

'Oh yes, you wouldn't hardly know she'd been so ill.'

Louise stayed a little longer, chatting about William's health, which had given no cause for alarm since his collapse on the train, and then walked on to pay a brief visit to her own home.

'Your Dad will run you back,' her mother said.

But Dr Weston was watching a nature programme on television and Louise could not bear to spoil such a rare treat.

'I don't mind the walk a bit and I'm not tired either. Good-night, Mum, I'll soon be back home again—I hope!'

She started out briskly, facing the wind now and noticing that it felt even more damp. It was certainly blowing up rain, as the local people called it. Wishing that she had put on her anorak instead of a cardigan, Louise quickened her pace.

And then it began to rain in earnest, beating into her face and making it difficult to keep her eyes open, so that she stumbled sometimes in the half-darkness. The pollarded willows on either side gave little protection and Louise kept to the middle of the road, uncomfortably aware of two deep ditches full of water.

Hurrying along, with her head down, she was suddenly completely blinded by the undipped lights of a car's headlamps coming towards her.

The road was narrow, little more than a track, and the only way she could escape the car's inexorable approach was by leaping towards the bank. She landed badly and slipped, and, clinging desperately to tufts of grass, felt both her shoes filling with water. The car swept past without slackening its speed, reached the village and vanished. Mark must have been summoned urgently to Marchester, Louise reasoned as she scrambled back to safety.

Miserably wet and extremely cross, she was busily engaged in emptying her shoes when she heard the car coming back, the driver having presumably turned round where there was more room. Dazzling brilliance again enveloped her, but this time the speed was much less and she dared to stand her ground.

'Get in.' Mark leaned across and flung open the passenger's door. 'It's lucky I glimpsed you when I passed before or I wouldn't have known where to look. Why on earth were you hiding?'

'Hiding?' Louise gasped at the effrontery of it and made no attempt to get in. 'I wasn't doing anything of the sort. I was merely trying to avoid being mown down.' She fastened the second shoe and stood up with bedraggled dignity. 'Anyway, I couldn't possibly accept a lift. I'm far too wet.'

'Rubbish!' His tone changed. 'Unless, of course, you'd prefer to walk back in the rain?'

Put like that, it sounded absurd and Louise gave in. They drove on for a moment in silence and then Mark asked her how she had got on with Mrs Taunton.

'She's willing to come and work for you, provided it's only for a short time. She wants you to call for her at half-eight tomorrow morning, if it's convenient.'

'I shall have to make it convenient.' Mark changed gear as they neared the end of the road. 'It's very strange that nobody seems to want to spend much time at Creek House—except Anna, of course. You, for instance, have made it very plain that you can hardly wait to get away.'

'It's not the house—not in my case, anyway.' Louise came to an abrupt halt.

'What is it then?'

'Oh, lots of things.' She was deliberately vague, since it was impossible to tell her employer—who had apparently got his car out specially to rescue her from the rain—that she didn't like either him or his housekeeper. 'I've agreed to stay until Vicky is better, so let's drop the subject, shall we?'

'Very well,' he said curtly.

But it was Louise who couldn't leave it alone.

'I expect you'll be glad to get Creek House back to normal,' she found herself saying. 'You came here for peace and quiet, didn't you? Those two items have been in pretty short supply just lately and you must be looking forward to having the place to yourselves again, you and Vicky—and Anna.'

She was annoyed with herself as soon as she had spoken and not surprised when Mark made no reply. They had reached the house and he swept up the short drive and round to the side. The rain had almost stopped and, as Louise stepped out, she saw a young moon struggling free of the clouds. It shone down on the marshes, turning the water to silver, and she paused, caught by the loveliness, and suddenly strangely anxious to share it with someone.

There was no one but Mark and she turned to him impulsively. 'Isn't it lovely! The marshes are so beautiful by moonlight.'

'I thought you hated them,' he said in surprise.

'Oh no!' The suggestion had shocked her. 'I've known them all my life and I love them, but I wouldn't want to live as close as this. They can be very frightening sometimes.'

'Dangerous too. I hope you aren't in the habit of wandering about by yourself?'

She was scornful of his warning. 'Of course I do, but I'm always very careful. We were brought up to treat the marshes with respect but we were never forbidden to go there once we were old enough to be sensible.'

'I suppose it's okay when you grow up with a really intimate knowledge of the dangers,' Mark said thoughtfully. 'But I certainly hope Vicky'll never go wandering off by herself.'

'I don't think there's much danger of that— not yet, anyway.'

Louise had walked to the edge of the lawn and Mark followed her there. They stood side by side, their arms not quite touching, staring out across the watery waste. And suddenly it seemed to her that the tension between them had totally vanished. For no reason at all she had stopped disliking him. For the moment.

It was Mark who broke the silence. 'Do you understand now why I left Marchester and came to live here? Just compare this with the noise of city streets and the feeling of having your life entirely dominated by the hospital— the never-ending talk of shop and all the petty gossip. Don't you think it's worth the drive morning and evening to escape all that?'

'Yes, I suppose so.' Louise answered automatically, her attention caught by the word *gossip*. Had they talked about his relationship with Anna? Was that what he really meant? 'I must go in and see if Vicky is all right.' She turned away abruptly.

She found the child sleeping and touched her forehead gently. It was cool and slightly damp, and she felt sure that the worst was over. Tomorrow Vicky would be convalescent. In a few days she would be back at play school and her nurse would be able to resume her interrupted holiday. Anna would have to manage as best she could.

But it didn't work out like that at all.

Louise was up early in the morning and she visited her patient without stopping to dress first. Vicky was awake and complaining of hunger—a very good sign indeed—but when Louise went down to the kitchen she was puzzled by the total silence in the house. It was nearly eight o'clock and Mark should have been stirring.

Had he forgotten that he had to call for Mrs Taunton at half-past?

She boiled an egg for the little girl, cut soldiers of thin bread and butter, and made some tea for herself. When she had arranged it all on a tray she hesitated. Perhaps Mark would appreciate a cup? Deciding that it might help him to get up, she poured one out and carried her burden carefully upstairs.

His door was still closed and she tapped on it and stood listening, uncertain whether the croaking sound she had heard was an invitation to enter or not. Making up her mind to risk it, she turned the handle slowly, giving him plenty of time to tell her to get out.

Nothing happened and she called to him again. 'I've brought you some tea, Doctor.'

Inside the room it was almost dark. The curtains were fully drawn and Louise could only see a hunched figure in the bed, the blankets pulled up high. 'What's the time?' asked a muffled voice.

'It's past eight and you promised to collect Mrs Taunton.'

'Oh no—' He struggled into a sitting position and groaned. 'I'd forgotten her. I can't possibly go—I've got that damn bug of Vicky's and I feel like death.'

He looked like it too. Now that she had grown accustomed to the gloom, Louise could see his black-shadowed eyes, bright with fever, and a pale face partly hidden by dark stubble.

'Oh dear!' she exclaimed involuntarily. 'It seems you'll have to stay in bed. Would you like me to ring the hospital and tell them you won't be in?'

'Certainly not—I've no intention of staying in bed. I'll rest a little longer and then get off to Marchester as usual.'

'Giving the virus to everybody you come across during the day?'

He brushed aside the interrruption. 'I'm afraid I can't possibly get to the village in time to pick up Mrs What's-her-name. Can you drive?'

'Yes, but—'

'You're not to take my car. There's another in the garage which Anna uses when she hasn't got a broken ankle.' He broke off to struggle with a fit of coughing and then peered at the cup which Louise still held in her hand. 'What's that?'

When she repeated that she had brought him some tea, he took it from her with no appearance of gratitude and drank it down thirstily.

'You'd better be dosed with something,' she said, rescuing the cup and saucer from a shaking hand. 'Is there some paracetamol in the bathroom cupboard?'

Interpreting his grunt as an affirmative, she fetched the tablets and stood over him while he swallowed them. Resisting an impulse to tidy the bed, she went away to dress and then hurried downstairs to find Anna.

The Danish girl was coming slowly out of the dining-room on her crutches. 'I have not slept well,' she announced. 'That camp bed is no good.'

'Sorry about that!' Louise produced a smile

to soften the retort. 'Listen, Anna—I need your car keys as I have to fetch the cleaning woman.' She added a brief description of Dr Halliwell's condition. 'He says he's going to Marchester but he's certainly not fit.'

'He must not go—it would be crazy! He could so easily have an accident with the car. You must stop him, Louise!' Anna finished dramatically.

'I have a feeling his own physical condition will do that as soon as he tries to get up. He's already very sorry for himself.'

'Men are always so when they are ill.'

Louise made no comment although she agreed heartily. It had suddenly occurred to her that it looked as though she had acquired another patient at Creek House. Once more her departure was likely to be delayed.

CHAPTER FOUR

'DEAR, DEAR!' Mrs Taunton said sympathetically. 'You've got your hands full at Creek House, Miss Weston, and no mistake.'

Louise carefully reversed the car and headed back towards the marshes. 'Having the doctor in bed will certainly make things much more complicated, since Anna can do practically nothing.'

'I reckon he'll expect to have a fuss made of him. It's my experience men usually feel that way when they're ill.'

It was impossible to imagine Mark wanting to be made a fuss of and Louise repressed a wry smile. In any case, she had no intention of attempting it.

'He said he was going to Marchester as usual,' she told Mrs Taunton, 'but I don't think he'll be able to.'

She was right about that. When they reached the house, Anna reported that Mark had staggered downstairs fully dressed and gone out to the garage, but he had returned almost at once and announced that he was spending the day in bed. At his request she had phoned his registrar and explained the situation.

'So terrible he looked,' she said to Louise, 'and he was shivering from head to foot though it is not at all cold this morning.'

Returning to Vicky's room, Louise glanced at Mark's closed door as she passed. Perhaps she ought to check that he was all right?

She opened the door cautiously and saw the same humped figure she had seen before. The only difference was that his pyjamas lay on the floor and there was no sign of daytime clothing scattered around.

With an exclamation of disapproval she crossed to the bed. 'Why on earth have you still got all your clothes on?'

'I was cold,' he mumbled, 'and I couldn't be bothered to undress.'

'You'll be much more comfortable in your pyjamas. If I go downstairs and fetch you a hot water bottle, will you get into bed properly while I'm gone?'

'No,' he said curtly. 'Leave me alone, Louise, for God's sake. You're not *my* nurse.'

'I know that, and I'm grateful for it,' she retorted. 'But unfortunately I've got a conscience and it's telling me right now that I ought to take your temperature. I suppose it's no good suggesting it?'

'None whatsoever.'

'As I thought.' She pulled up the blankets,

ignoring his muttered protests, and went away.

Vicky had now reached the demanding stage of convalescence and Louise spent much of the day reading to her and playing simple games. She did not go near the child's father until another dose of tablets became due.

Mark seemed to be dozing when she went in but he immediately opened his eyes and fixed Louise with a reproachful stare.

'Nobody's been near me for hours,' he complained. 'For all you knew I might have been dying.'

'I didn't think it was likely,' she said sweetly. 'And you said you wanted to be left alone. I only came in now to remind you to take another dose of paracetamol.'

She fetched some fresh water for him and stood over him again as he gulped the tablets down. 'Would you like another cup of tea?' she asked.

'I'd rather have beer—ice cold from the fridge. I'm just as hot now as I was cold earlier.'

'That's quite usual with a temperature, as you must know.'

'Of course I know! Are you going to fetch that beer or not?'

'Not. But I'll bring you some orange juice.'

Taking no notice of his indignation, Louise went downstairs and found Anna in the kitchen, sitting wearily at the table and doing nothing.

'How is he?'

'The bug is running its course but I think he'll live.' She opened the fridge door and searched for orange juice.

'You think he'll live?' Anna's sapphire blue eyes widened in alarm. 'You make a joke— yes?' And when Louise confirmed it she added reproachfully, 'It is not kind to laugh at a sick man.'

'I wasn't really laughing at him.' She glanced at the Danish girl thoughtfully. 'I expect you wish you could get up the stairs to see how the doctor is for yourself. Maybe he'd let you look after him properly, but he certainly won't let me. I could make him a lot more comfortable if only he'd co-operate.'

There was a long pause and then Anna sighed. 'It is hard for me to be a prisoner here and Mark ill in his room. We have been friends for some time and understand each other. It may be that he would have preferred to be tended by someone he knows well rather than a stranger.'

It was very much the sort of reply that Louise had expected; nevertheless, she found it strangely unwelcome and she answered rather more sharply than she had intended.

'It's a pity that you hurt your ankle. If it hadn't been for that I wouldn't have had to

come here at all. You could have looked after
Vicky and coped with her father as well. I'm
sure you'd be perfectly capable of it.'

'I would have done my best,' Anna said with
dignity.

It had been an unsatisfactory exchange and
Louise retreated back upstairs. Vicky was now
progressing so rapidly that she found it difficult
to keep her amused.

'You can go downstairs tomorrow,' she
promised, 'and I think you'll be able to go back
to play school soon. You'll like that, won't
you?'

'Yes,' Vicky said decisively. 'Do you think I
gave my germs to any of the other children like
I did Daddy?'

'I don't know, but I expect you'll find out
when you get back.'

'Daddy's never ill. Is he very cross with me
for making him ill now?'

'He hasn't said so, and you couldn't help it.'

'Do you think you'll catch it too?' Vicky
asked with interest.

Louise smiled and shook her head. 'Nurses
don't catch things as easily as other people.
They know how to look after themselves.'

'I'd like to be a nurse when I grow up. It
must be lovely not to catch horrid germs.'

It was an original reason for taking up
nursing and they discussed it at length before
tackling a jigsaw puzzle. When the time came

for another dose of paracetamol, Louise felt that the day had been going on ever since she could remember. Was it really only this morning that she had discovered Mark was ill?

This time she found him in bed properly, his clothes flung about the floor. He accepted the tablets with surprising meekness and made no comment when she lingered to tidy the room. Studying his appearance as unobtrusively as possible, she longed yet again to fetch the thermometer from the bathroom.

'Have you taken your temperature?' she asked in a carefully casual tone.

'No. And I don't intend to—or to let you take it either.'

'You're a rotten doctor when it's yourself who is the patient. You made me keep a proper chart of Vicky's temperature.'

'It's different with a child, but I know darned well I've got a high temperature and I'm not interested in finding out what it is to the nearest decimal point.'

Louise left it at that, replenished his fruit juice and went away again. When she looked in at bedtime he appeared to be sleeping heavily and she did not disturb him.

In the early hours of the morning she awoke suddenly, convinced that some sound had penetrated her consciousness. Had Vicky called out? She was sitting up in bed when the noise came again—stumbling steps on the landing outside her door.

Switching on the lamp with one hand, Louise reached out for her dressing-gown with the other. It was certainly not Vicky who was up and about at that hour, and when she opened her door she saw Mark standing there, illuminated by a shaft of moonlight from the window. He looked at her vaguely and ran a hand through his untidy hair.

'Thought I heard the phone.'

'I don't think it rang. You must have been dreaming about the hospital.' Louise went up to him and put a hand on his arm. Through the thin cotton pyjama sleeve it felt burning hot. 'Come back to bed now, Doctor, *please*.'

He allowed her to steer him back to his room and made no protest when she pushed him gently into an armchair.

'This is a good opportunity to make your bed more comfortable.'

Swiftly, with practised hands, she straightened and smoothed the sheets and plumped up the pillows. Leaning back against a cushion, Mark watched her with half-closed eyes.

'You look very efficient in spite of the green velvet caftan,' he observed. 'I should think when you're in uniform you could strike terror into the most hostile patient.'

Louise laughed. 'I hope I'm never as fierce as that! Anyway, I very rarely have hostile patients. Most people are very willing to be looked after when they're ill.'

'Was that aimed at me?'

'If you like.' She tucked in one side of the bed and opened the other invitingly. 'There you are—it's all ready for you.'

But Mark showed no sign of moving. 'I was asleep most of the day and now I feel wide awake, if a little light-headed. And I know that's due to my temperature, so you don't have to tell me.'

'I wasn't going to. I've entirely lost interest in your temperature.'

'Really? That's a very wrong attitude for a nurse.'

'I can't help that.' She smiled. 'Is there anything you'd like me to get you before I go back to bed, Doctor?'

She was standing very near and, to her surprise, he reached out and caught her hand.

'There's nothing I want you to *get*, but I'd like you to do two things. Stop calling me Doctor—and stay and talk to me for a little while.'

'All right—er—Mark, just for a few minutes.'

Aware that fever could do strange things to people, Louise struggled to remain totally detached, to accept his friendliness clinically and not attach the slightest importance to it. She glanced down disapprovingly at his bare feet and continued in a strictly professional tone.

'But I must insist on one condition—that you get into bed. You're running the risk of a chill sitting there in your pyjamas.'

'As you say, Nurse.' He meekly did as he was told, lying down with a long weary sigh.

Louise resisted an extraordinary impulse to smooth the tumbled hair from his hot forehead, and sat down in the chair he had vacated. 'What shall we talk about?'

'You choose,' Mark murmured lazily.

'How about Vicky then? Don't you want a progress report? You haven't asked after her all day but I expect you've been feeling too ill to bother.'

'I knew you were taking good care of her,' he said disarmingly. 'I expect she's on the mend now, isn't she?'

'Oh yes. She started to get better quite suddenly and I think she's looking forward to going back to play school.' Louise hesitated. 'She seems rather a lonely little girl,' she ventured.

His eyes opened wide and held her reproachful gaze with a steely glare. 'Meaning that I'm a rotten father? You could be right but it's not because I don't try.'

'Well, it did just cross my mind that an awful lot of your time is devoted to caring for other people's children at, perhaps, the expense of your own—' She broke off in consternation as

Mark made a violent movement and shot up in
bed.

'Vicky's *not* my child! And because of that
I've never been able to give her the affection
she ought to have, poor little kid. It's not her
fault and it's wicked she should have to suffer
for it, but somehow I just can't feel towards
her the way I know I ought.'

Shocked at the volcano of emotion which
she had innocently caused to erupt, Louise sat
quietly with folded hands and waited for him
to continue. Mark, too, was silent for a moment and then he went rushing on.

'There's nothing unusual about the story.
What my—my wife did to me has been done
plenty of times, but that doesn't stop me calling it a filthy trick. I was a junior registrar at the
time and Jenny was a student nurse. We fell in
love—and with me it was for real. We
embarked on a passionate affair which she
apparently tired of quite soon. Unknown to
me, she took up with some other bloke—
nobody who worked at the hospital or I would
have heard about it.'

'Had you no suspicion at all?' Louise asked
in surprise.

'None—I was completely fooled, though
eventually, of course, the penny dropped sufficiently for me to realise she'd cooled off.
Then she came to me in great distress, said she
was pregnant and asked me what I was going to

do about it. She didn't want a termination, even if she could have got one, and so I was trapped into marriage. Only I didn't know it was a trap then.'

'It was the other man who'd got her pregnant?'

'Exactly. We had a furious row one day, not long before Vicky was born, and my wife taunted me with the truth.'

Even after nearly five years his eyes were dark with pain as he relived that long-ago scene. Genuinely sympathetic as she was, Louise could not understand why he still clung to that sense of betrayal. Or was it because Vicky was a constant reminder?

'Anna told me your wife died in childbirth,' she said quietly. 'That's rather unusual these days.'

'Jenny had a severe haemorrhage and her blood group was a rare one. It was before I came to Marchester and the small local hospital had problems getting sufficient.'

It was a sad story and Louise felt it was better to make no further comment on it. Mark probably wouldn't have told her if the circumstances hadn't been out of the ordinary. Experience had taught her that patients were more likely to unburden themselves in the middle of the night.

'Vicky is a nice little girl,' she said at last. 'Maybe one day you'll get to know her better.'

'Perhaps. I haven't had much chance so far. She was brought up by a nanny, and then when she was four Anna came and the two of them got on well right from the start. Vicky doesn't need me.'

'I disagree.'

'She's a lot happier than children sometimes are in one-parent families,' Mark insisted. 'She's got Anna, who's here all the time instead of having to leave her with a childminder and go out to earn a living.'

'But Anna isn't her mother—' Louise broke off and bit her lip.

Maybe, one day, Anna would become Vicky's mother—and what could be more suitable?

Mark was looking desperately tired. He slid down in the bed again and glanced across at Louise. 'I can feel another shivering fit coming on. Would you mind going down to the kitchen and getting me a hot drink?'

Astonished at the polite wording of the request, she sprang to her feet. 'Of course I don't mind. What would you like?'

He chose tea and she tiptoed carefully down the steep stairs, anxious that Anna shouldn't wake up and—perhaps—place a wrong interpretation on the situation.

The electric kettle boiled quickly and she was soon back, taking the teapot with her in case Mark wanted a second cup, and also a cup for herself. He was lying as she had left him, his eyes closed and the lamp throwing deep shadows on to his lean face.

He accepted the drink with gratitude and praised her forethought in bringing the pot. He was completely and utterly different from the man she had hitherto known.

'Thanks for letting me talk, Louise,' he said when she had tidied up and was ready to leave.

'I'm glad I now understand the situation a little better,' she told him sincerely. 'But I still hope that as time goes on you'll feel less bitter and somehow come to terms with what happened.'

His lips twisted into a rueful smile. 'I can see you're set on a happy ending, but I'm making no promises. In my experience life doesn't go in much for neatness.'

She was standing close to him, about to pick up the tray from the bedside table, when he made a sudden grab at her hand, just as he had done earlier.

'Is there something else you want?' she asked.

'Yes—but I know I'm not going to get it. Your hygenic principles would never permit such a thing.'

'I wish I knew what you're on about,' Louise said uneasily.

Mark smiled a genuine smile, without bitterness of any sort. 'You look so very attractive in

that green garment, and you've been keeping
your prickles so marvellously out of sight that
I'd very much like to kiss you good-night. But I
know it would be crazy with me in this filthy
state of germiness. So—' hot dry lips were
suddenly pressed into her palm—'that will
have to do for the present. Good-night,
Louise—and thank you again.'

'Good-night, Mark,' she managed to say
sedately before almost fleeing from the room
to seek sanctuary in her own.

Illness certainly had a very strange effect on
some people. Sitting on the bed with the tray
on her lap, Louise stared into space and tried
to still her racing pulse. Mark would certainly
regret it in the morning. Unless, of course, he
forgot the whole thing or decided it had been
an attack of delirium, which would definitely
be preferable.

As for her own feelings, one thing was clear.
The sooner she escaped from Creek House the
better.

CHAPTER FIVE

LOUISE AWOKE the following morning with an odd feeling that something important had happened. Yet when she remembered the events of the night she couldn't understand why they should seem of any great significance. It had been pleasant to see her employer in a different mood, and she felt honoured by his confidences regarding Vicky's mother, but she didn't believe the improvement in their relationship was likely to continue.

She was right about that. When she went in to find out if he wanted anything she saw only a hunched shoulder and the back of a dark head.

'All I want is to be left in peace,' said a muffled voice, 'if it wouldn't be too much trouble.'

'Not half as much trouble as supplying you with orange juice and cups of tea, to say nothing of forcing you to take your medicine,' Louise told him tartly.

'I don't need any more of your dosing. My temperature's probably normal this morning.'

'I'm glad to hear it. Does that mean you'll be fetching your own requirements in future?'

'Certainly—when I get around to wanting anything to eat and drink.'

Disapproving, but knowing it would be useless to protest, Louise left him, as he had desired, in peace. When she gave Anna an edited version of the conversation the Danish girl shrugged in disgust.

'Men! They are so childish when they are ill. If Mark is over the worst he should have light, nourishing food. If only I could climb the stairs I would see that he got it.'

'I expect you know how to handle him.'

'But of course. As I told you, we are good friends, the doctor and I.'

The conversation ended there and Louise concentrated on preparing Vicky's breakfast. If Mark came down later on she knew nothing about it, for it was a brilliantly sunny day and she allowed her little patient to get up and go out into the garden.

'The grass wants cutting,' Vicky observed.

'Who usually does it?'

'Sometimes Daddy, sometimes Anna.'

'Neither of them can possibly attend to it at present. What sort of mower is it?'

On learning that it was electric, she located it in a shed and, instructed by Vicky, connected up the cable and plugged it into the nearest power point. Walking up and down the sloping lawn was strangely soothing and relieved some of her pent-up energy. Taking it by and large, she reflected, this nursing job was just about the most unsatisfactory she had ever undertaken.

'That's not what you're getting paid for,' said a voice over the hedge.

'Dad!' Louise switched off and ran to greet him. 'What on earth are you doing here?'

'I had a few minutes to spare so I thought I'd drive down the creek road and take a look at the marshes. I thought I might be lucky enough to see some interesting birds but I didn't expect to see you doing a bit of gardening.'

Louise laughed. 'I'm quite enjoying it, actually, and Vicky is almost well now.'

'Does that mean you'll be home soon?'

'Either tomorrow or the day after.'

James Weston looked at his daughter thoughtfully from beneath grey, jutting eyebrows. Sensing that he had something on his mind, Louise asked him what it was.

'That agency woman rang up yesterday. Said she'd got an urgent job you might be interested in and you were to phone her when you got home.'

'But she knows I'm on holiday! I don't want to take on another job just yet. Did she give any details?'

'No, but your mother promised you'd contact her so you'd better do it.' He looked at his watch. 'I must be on my way. Glad to have seen you, dear.'

He drove off in his usual impetuous fashion, sending the dust flying in his wake, and Louise looked after him affectionately. He was a very knowledgeable ornithologist and it was a shame he had so little time for his hobby when the marshes were such a good place for bird-watching, and so near at hand.

'I don't want to cut any more grass,' Vicky said.

'You mean you don't want *me* to cut any more?' Louise smiled and ruffled the fair hair with a gentle hand. 'Let's sit under that tree and I'll read to you.'

The day passed slowly, as had most of the time Louise had spent at Creek House. Following her instructions strictly, she kept away from Mark's room and saw nothing of him at all, although Anna reported that he had announced he was returning to work tomorrow.

'It is too soon,' she said emphatically, making her clicking sound of disapproval.

'Did you tell him so?" Louise asked.

'Most certainly, but he would not listen.' Anna put her arm round Vicky and drew the child to her. 'And how is my little one? Quite better now?'

'Almost quite. I'm going back to work tomorrow too.'

'I suppose you mean play school? I think you'd better wait one more day and then you can return to school and I can go home,' Louise put in.

Vicky left Anna's encircling arm and came to rub her head against Louise's. 'I don't want you to go. Can't you stay here until Anna can walk properly again?'

'Goodness—no! I wouldn't have any nursing to do and I should hate that.' She touched the petal-smooth cheek gently with her finger. 'I shall miss you, Vicky, but I really can't stay any longer.'

'I shall miss *you*.' Large eyes gazed up innocently into her face. 'And so will Daddy. He won't have anybody to talk to in the middle of the night.'

There was a horrible silence as both girls stared at the child, and then Anna burst into speech.

'I don't understand! What is this you are saying, Vicky?'

'I woke up and I heard Daddy talking to Nurse, and then they went into his room and I heard the door shut.'

There was no reason in the world why Louise should feel guilty; nevertheless she was furiously aware that her colour had deepened. Anna's lips had tightened and she was clearly waiting for an explanation, but it was to the little girl that Louise addressed it.

'Your Daddy thought he heard the phone ring and got up. I think his high temperature was making him feel a bit funny—just like it did you. I heard somebody stumbling about on the landing and went to see who it was.'

'Go on, Louise,' Anna said levelly. 'This is very interesting. So what happened then?'

'He said he'd like a cup of tea and I went downstairs and made some. That's all.'

Anna plainly didn't believe that it was. 'Did you also drink tea?' she demanded.

Louise's eyebrows rose. 'I can't see it matters whether I did or not, but if you really want to know—yes, I did have a cup and Dr Halliwell had two. Does that satisfy you?'

She had made it clear from her tone that it was all the explanation she intended to give, and Anna was obliged to accept it. But it was impossible not to be aware that their relationship—never very cordial—had deteriorated. The only thing on which they now seemed to be in accord was their united disapproval of Mark's insistence on going to Marchester in the morning.

He departed, silent and morose, but Louise—observing that Vicky still looked a little frail—decided that she must wait another day before leaving. A phone call to the play school ensured that someone would give the child a lift for the time being, and with that taken care of there was nothing to do but get through the day as best she could. Mark was late back and she saw little of him. After a silent meal with Anna she retired to her room.

In the morning Vicky was pleased to be returning to school and said goodbye quite cheerfully. Outside in the fresh morning air, Louise drew a deep breath of relief and paused for a moment to stare out across the marshes. There were little rippling noises from the creeks, and in the distance a line of greyish-blue indicated the presence of a much vaster volume of water—the sea.

'How are you getting home?' asked Mark's voice abruptly.

Louise started and spun round. He had backed his car out of the garage and had apparently been doing something to the engine, for the bonnet was up.

'I thought you'd gone!' she exclaimed involuntarily.

'I've been checking the oil and a few other items.' He was wiping his hands on a tissue. 'Will you answer my question, please.'

'I intend to walk. My case isn't heavy and I didn't think I ought to bother my father.'

'Why didn't you ask me to drive you? Surely I'm the obvious person.'

Louise shrugged and resisted the temptation to tell him he was the least obvious person she'd ever come across. Mark finished cleaning his hands and opened the passenger's door.

'I hope you're not going to start arguing. I haven't got all day,' he said tersely.

She tightened her lips and got in, determined not to delay him a single moment since there was apparently no escape from the unwanted lift.

'I expect you're glad to be going,' he said abruptly as they swept down the road.

'I'm certainly not sorry. Vicky is a dear little girl and I enjoyed looking after her, but she didn't really want much nursing and I prefer a tougher sort of job.'

'I would have thought most of your jobs were very easy. Aren't you usually employed by the idle rich who probably don't need much nursing either?'

'The idle rich!' Louise did not trouble to hide her scorn. 'That's an out-dated expression if ever I heard one. People have to work very hard indeed if they want to become—and remain—rich these days. And they can get just as seriously ill as anyone else.'

Mark did not reply and she stole a glance at his profile. Outlined against a pale blue sky it looked angular and uncompromising, and she thought how clearly it defined his personality. There was nothing soft about him anywhere, nothing gentle or tender—he was granite right through.

The silence lasted until the car was approaching Holly Lodge.

'Thank you for the lift,' Louise said politely.

'I don't suppose we shall meet again.' Mark ignored the small courtesy. 'You'll be off to some exotic foreign place as soon as your holiday is finished.'

'Perhaps, but all my jobs haven't been abroad. As a matter of fact—' She hesitated, wondering why she was on the verge of becoming confidential. Obviously he wouldn't be interested. 'I've asked for a hospital job as my next assignment. You're in danger of getting out of touch, nursing private patients all the time.'

'In London?'

'It's the most likely place, and I like the big London hospitals. You really feel you're at the heart of the medical world there.'

'Rubbish!' Mark snorted.

Louise turned an astonished face towards him. 'What do you mean?'

His answer came fiercely. 'Many of the provincial hospitals are just as up to date—and some are actually pioneers in one way or another.' And he added explosively, 'I can't stand medical snobbery.'

She would have liked to continue the discussion but they had now reached her home and she knew he was eager to be off. His hand was already on the gear lever as she thanked him again and jumped out quickly without a backward glance.

Yet as she walked up the drive she was aware that Mark had not yet driven away. The car was still stationary at the gate. Puzzled, she paused on the doorstep and looked over her shoulder. His face was turned towards her and he had obviously been watching her backview.

Feeling vaguely that some gesture was required, Louise waved her hand. And immediately the car shot violently up the road with a roar from the exhaust, as though he now couldn't get away quickly enough. Extraordinary man!

Indoors, she found her mother busy in the kitchen where she was making strawberry jam. Although pleased to see Louise back, she needed no assistance.

'Don't forget to ring the agency,' she called as Louise drifted away.

'I'll wait until this afternoon. It's so expensive to phone London in the morning. Did you take the message when Mrs Acland called?'

'Yes, but it's no good asking me for the details because she didn't give any.' Marion Weston turned a flushed face towards her. 'I hope you won't go rushing off just yet, dear. You haven't nearly finished your holiday.'

'I don't expect I shall accept another job immediately, unless there's something very special about it, but I'd better see what she wants.'

As the time for telephoning approached,

her curiosity increased. For some reason the morning had seemed very long and empty. She had expected to resume her holiday with a feeling of immense contentment after her experiences at Creek House, but it wasn't like that at all. There was too little to do and too much time for doing it.

Immediately after lunch she was in the hall, dialling the agency number.

'I know you've got another week's leave,' Mrs Acland said in her brisk voice, 'but I've had an urgent request for a couple of nurses to help out during the holiday season at a general hospital. I remembered you said you'd like a hospital job but there's another reason why you came straight into my mind.'

'What's that?' Louise asked in surprise.

'The hospital in question is in your area. It's the one at Marchester where you trained and I'm sure you'd enjoy going back for a few weeks. You could live at home, I should imagine, and travel to the city daily. It isn't far, is it?'

'About fifteen miles. I—I hardly know what to say, Mrs Acland.' Her mind in a turmoil, Louise tried to think of some acceptable way of postponing her decision. It had never even occurred to her that she might be offered a post at her old hospital. Coming out of the blue like that it had been not merely a surprise but a considerable shock.

'You're surely not hesitating? In my opinion it's a lucky break for you and I assumed you'd be delighted,' the voice at the other end exclaimed impatiently.

'Oh yes, of course I am, Mrs Acland, but—well, there are a few problems. For instance, I'd have a very real difficulty with transport. I haven't a car of my own and the bus only runs twice daily.'

'There's a train, isn't there? From Deenham Market, I believe.'

'Yes, that's right, but I'd still have to get to the station.'

'I'm sure you've got a bicycle, dear, and an early morning ride in the summer ought to be quite enjoyable. Can I take it as settled then?'

Louise clutched the receiver, hating the feeling of being rushed. Yet she had often in the past had to make up her mind quickly about a job and she had never minded before. On the face of it there was no reason in the world why she shouldn't want to go to Marchester General.

'Well?' demanded Mrs Acland with a return of her impatience. 'Is it settled?'

'I—I suppose so. I'm sorry I've been dithering but—well—' Louise left the sentence unfinished. 'You don't know what ward I shall be sent to?' she added a little breathlessly.

'Good gracious, no! That's a matter for the hospital to decide. It's not important, surely?'

'Oh no—I just felt curious, that's all. Who's the other nurse you're sending to Marchester?'

'Celia Browning, but I don't think you know her. She's a very nice girl and I'm sure you'll like each other. Goodbye now, dear. I'll send you a confirmation by post and you can expect to start next Monday.'

Louise slackened her frenzied grip of the receiver and replaced it thoughtfully, but she did not immediately go and report to her mother. She needed a brief interlude in the peaceful hall to come to terms with what had just happened and she spent the time in enumerating all the many advantages.

She would enjoy living at home—for a time anyway—and it would be interesting to return to her old hospital and discover all the changes that had taken place. They were in the midst of a grand building programme, her father had told her, and she might even find trouble in making her way around.

As she had expected, her parents were delighted that they were to have her at home for several more weeks. Her father even found time to examine her old bicycle and make sure it was in working order.

'It only needs oiling,' he said, using his car pump on the tyres, 'and a bit of cleaning too, of course.'

Louise washed off some very dry mud and struggled with the sense of unreality. Only a short time ago she had been in Corsica, being driven about in a Rolls on the rare occasions when her patient felt well enough to go out. And now she was proposing to ride a bicycle to Deenham Station again, just as she had done in her school days.

On Monday morning she was up early, glad to see it was fine. Her blue staff nurse's uniform had been beautifully washed, starched and ironed by skilled hands before she came home, and she wondered if it would ever look as perfect again. Her frilly cap was stiffly starched too and she put it carefully into a polythene bag which she slung from the handlebars. A navy cardigan hid the bright red belt and made her feel less conspicuous.

The sense of unreality was still with her when she joined the commuters on the platform and waited for her train, and when she eventually walked in at the main entrance of the hospital she had difficulty in recognising any of it.

A miniature roundabout sorted out the traffic and there was a huge new car park on the left. Ahead of her a big new block announced that it was the Outpatients and X-ray department. Further along she was relieved to see something familiar—the central entrance was just as she remembered it, although other new buildings and some still in the process of being built stretched away to the right.

At that early hour the office dealing with nursing staff was only occupied by a couple of clerks.

'Nurse Weston? I should have your name on a list somewhere, I think.' The girl began to turn over pages with a practised hand.

As Louise waited she was aware of increasing nervousness. She really didn't mind at all which ward they sent her to—with one exception—but she knew perfectly well that fate frequently delighted in playing tricks.

'Here we are,' said the clerk suddenly. 'Sinclair ward. That's a male surgical ward. If you follow the signs you'll have no difficulty in finding it.'

Louise followed them thankfully. Fate hadn't played a trick after all and she was well content with her assignment. On the whole she preferred surgical nursing to medical and she felt sure she would find the work interesting.

It was a long way, along corridors and up stairs and along more corridors, and she marvelled afresh at the huge place Marchester General had become.

There could be no possible doubt about the improbability of ever coming into contact with the paediatrician, or even catching a glimpse of him, since the children's ward, she had noted, lay in the opposite direction.

And that was the way she wanted it.

CHAPTER SIX

SINCLAIR was one of the older wards and Louise remembered it well. She had nursed there during her third year. There were long rows of beds and a desk at the top end instead of a proper nurses' station.

Sister McKinley was short and plump, with reddish hair slightly tinged with grey. She greeted the newcomer without enthusiasm and then looked pointedly at her watch.

'Is this the earliest you can get here, Staff Nurse?'

'I have a train journey first.'

'Good heavens! Well, I suppose it can't be helped and goodness knows I ought to be used to odd hours with so many part-timers, but I would have thought your agency might have sent me someone who could keep to the proper shifts. Can't you find somewhere to live in the city?'

'I'm sorry but I don't want to try,' Louise said firmly. 'The whole point of my coming here was so I could continue to live at home. I've been nursing abroad.'

'Oh, very well—we must just make the best of it, I suppose.' She beckoned another senior nurse. 'Take Nurse Weston round, Staff, and tell her what she needs to know about our patients. And then she'd better do a medicine round with you. Next time she will be on her own.'

'Why are you wearing a cap like mine?' Mary Denham, a slender dark girl, asked curiously.

Louise smiled. 'Because I qualified here and was a staff nurse for a short time.'

'And you've come back as a temp? You'll see a lot of changes.' She lowered her voice. 'Don't let Sister ruffle you—she's okay really but she worries a lot *and* she's got a weight problem. It makes her a bit short-tempered.'

The morning flew past, and during the brief moments when she had time to think at all Louise couldn't help comparing it with the way time had dragged at Creek House.

This was real nursing and it was satisfying to be once again involved with acute cases. They had a number of patients who had recently had operations of a severity and magnitude which she had not encountered for some time. As soon as Sister McKinley grasped that she was competent she was allocated several of them for her special care.

One was a boy of twenty named Robert Mason who had had a major abdominal operation from which he was clearly going to take a long time to recover. His name meant nothing to her at the time, but afterwards she realised that she should have recognised it.

She was off duty during the afternoon visiting hour and spent her time sitting in the nearby park watching the ducks on the pond. Her feet hadn't ached so much for years. After she returned to the hospital there was a breathless rush to get the evening toilet round dealt with, supper served and the ward tidied again for more visitors.

They poured in steadily, carrying flowers, paperback books and bundles of clean laundry. Among them there was a broad-shouldered young man who made straight for the bed just inside the door where Robert Mason, ashen-faced, lay propped up against pillows.

'Hi, Rob!' Louise heard him greet the patient. 'How're you doing then?'

There was something familiar about the voice, which was particularly clear and resonant, as though its owner might be a singer. Louise, on her way to check the blood pressure of a man who had been operated on that morning, paused and glanced at the visitor. She *had* heard that voice before, and she knew the profile too—the straight nose and jutting chin. She had once known it very well indeed.

She said nothing then, but on her return she stopped by Robert's bed.

'Hello, Colin.' Her smile was warm and friendly. 'It's a long time!'

'Louise!' His peculiarly brilliant blue eyes were alight with pleasure. 'It *is* a long time! What are you doing here? I thought you only took posh jobs now, nursing rich people on the Riviera and all that.'

'It begins to pall after a while and I thought I'd like a change. I've certainly got it here— this is a really tough ward.'

'I'll say!' His eyes went to the patient and his expression changed. 'Have you forgotten my little brother?'

'He was a schoolboy when I saw him last and so I didn't recognise him.' She moved closer to the bedside. 'Do you remember me, Robert? Your brother and I were both in the Deenham Operatic and Dramatic Society before your family moved to Marchester and I started my nursing training.'

'I remember you vaguely.' His voice was weak and uninterested.

'I only had small parts whereas Colin usually played lead.' Louise changed the subject. 'Are you quite comfortable or would you like another pillow?'

'As comfortable as I'm likely to be just now.'

A look of distress crossed Colin's face and then he turned back to Louise. 'When are you off duty? It might be fun to have a drink together and do a bit of reminiscing.'

The invitation was tempting but she hesitated nevertheless, thinking of the homeward journey. 'I've got to get back to Deenham and the trains aren't very frequent.'

'I'll drive you,' he said at once, and brushed aside her half-hearted protest, 'and we'll stop somewhere for a drink on the way.'

He was waiting for her outside the main door and they walked to the car park together, talking easily and cheerfully about the past they had briefly shared. It was not until they were in the car and had left the city traffic behind them that everything suddenly changed.

'Do you know about Rob?' Colin asked abruptly.

Louise was not quite sure what he meant but she knew she must be careful. Her own information was limited but she had certain suspicions which she intended to keep to herself.

But there was no need for caution.

Colin gave her no time to frame a reply to his question. Instead he went rushing on, the words pouring out as though he found relief in talking.

'I don't know how much they tell the nurses about the cases they're looking after. Probably as much as they need to know and no more. And so you may not be aware that my brother's got cancer.'

Louise made a small exclamation of distress. 'I wondered, but I wasn't sure—and of course I hoped he was okay.'

'Sister knows. She was there when the surgeon broke the news to my father and me.'

'What about your mother?'

'She's got a heart condition. They thought it better not to tell her at present.'

'It must be very hard not to let her guess there's something seriously wrong.'

Colin shook his head. A lock of fairish hair fell over his forehead and he brushed it back impatiently.

It was a small gesture which Louise remembered well and she felt a sudden strange upsurge of tenderness towards him. But whether it was due to sympathy because of his brother, or her own memories, she couldn't have said.

'I don't think it's even occurred to Mother that the boy's seriously ill, and Rob himself doesn't know, of course—though I believe he might have an inkling because he's so depressed. It's my bet he's wondering about it and is afraid to ask.'

'Could be.'

All Louise's pleasure at the reunion with an old friend had vanished and she felt tired and dispirited.

'Rob is one of my special patients,' she said thoughtfully. 'Would you like me to keep a look-out for signs of what's in his mind? Nurses have more chance of learning about patients' secret thoughts than their visitors do, even though they're family. Or because of it.'

'I'd be very grateful.' Colin's voice was slightly husky but he cleared his throat and continued in a determinedly brighter tone. 'It's high time we had that drink. We shall be at Deenham in a few minutes, so how about going to that pub where we used to gather after rehearsals?'

It was a good idea and Louise agreed at once. The place was packed and its warm, cheerful atmosphere at once dissipated the gloom which had accompanied them from Marchester. Louise found a small table vacant and sat down while Colin wormed his way to the bar. As she waited she looked round her.

The customers were a mixed bunch—farmers, farm workers, commuters and pensioners, and among them a number of young people who fitted into no category at all. Louise listened idly to the snippets of conversation which reached her and marvelled that an inn only a mile from the village where she had spent a large part of her life could contain so many total strangers.

But they weren't quite all strangers. It was as Colin was struggling towards her, carrying two glasses, that she heard a familiar voice.

Clear and slightly foreign, it cut suddenly through the hubbub around like the sharp blade of a knife slicing through butter. No one else seemed to notice but Louise half stood up and struggled to see round a group of people talking together in the middle of the floor.

Her efforts were unrewarded and she sank back into her seat just as Colin arrived. She thanked him mechanically, said 'Cheers!' in answer to his toast and helped herself to a handful of crisps. And just at that moment the crowd in front of them moved away in a body towards the door, leaving a clear space.

Anna sat in the opposite corner, her plastered ankle carefully stretched out. And, beside her, Mark. They were eating scampi and chips and drinking lager. They looked happy, relaxed and on very good terms with each other.

'This is nice,' Colin said contentedly. 'I'm glad you've come back to the neighbourhood, Louise.'

She turned her head towards him. 'You what?'

'I said I was glad you're back in circulation, *and* I meant it.'

'I think I'm going to like it too, though I never intended to stay when I came home for a holiday.' Resolutely Louise averted her eyes

from the couple opposite and gave him her full
attention. 'I rather hope I don't get itchy feet
any more for quite a while.'

'Have all your jobs been abroad?'

The subject lasted them for some time, but
in the middle of an animated description of the
decayed Italian palace where she had nursed a
dying opera singer, she was suddenly aware
that Anna's eyes were on her.

As she raised a nonchalant hand to give a
wave which included Mark as well, she wondered why he was staring at her so hard. There
was nothing out of the ordinary about visiting a
pub with a friend.

'Somebody you know?' Colin asked lightly.

'He's the children's doctor from the hospital. He lives at Barkington and I looked after
his little girl for a few days when she picked up
some sort of bug recently.'

'Why couldn't his wife nurse the child? Or
was it because of her ankle?'

'Anna isn't married to Dr Halliwell—she's
the housekeeper. And yes, it was because of
her fracture.'

Colin gave a hoot of mirth. 'Housekeeper?
You have to be joking!'

'That's what she's called, and she certainly
runs the house.'

'I bet that's not *all* she does.' He glanced
admiringly across at the Danish girl's blonde
hair and clear skin. 'I must say she's a good-

looker. That bloke knows how to pick 'em.'

The conversation was becoming increasingly distasteful to Louise, yet her escort had said nothing that any other man would not have said in similar circumstances and she felt bewildered by her own reaction. As she tried to think of something else to talk about she suddenly remembered the time.

'I shall have to go, Colin, or my mother will think I've missed the train. Thanks for the drink.'

'Can't you stay long enough to have another?'

'No—sorry. I really must go.'

'I'll drive you home.' He stood up reluctantly.

'You can drive me to the station to fetch my bike, if you like, though it's only a few hundred yards so it doesn't really matter. I can't possibly leave it there because I shall want it in the morning.

Another group of customers had entered and the only clear route to the door took them past the table where Anna and Mark sat. As they reached it Anna looked up and Louise felt impelled to pause and ask after her ankle.

'It is doing as well as can be expected. Is that what you say?' She grimaced and shrugged at the same time.

'And how's Vicky?'

Her eyes were on Mark as she put the question and it was he who answered.

'She's quite fit now.'

Louise had certainly not intended to ask her next question and until that moment she had never even thought of the possibility that Vicky might have been left by herself in the lonely house. But somehow she heard herself saying causally, 'I suppose you've got a baby-sitter?'

'Of course.' His gaze held hers, hard and brilliant and scornful. 'Does that surprise you? Did you imagine we hadn't bothered?'

'I hadn't thought about it at all until just now.' Louise held her head high, though her cheeks blazed with angry colour. 'It was only a—a conversational question and I'm sorry I asked it, since you seem to have taken exception to it.'

'Mrs Taunton consented to come in for a short time,' Anna put in. 'I was so weary of the house and Mark said he would take me out for a meal to cheer me up. The food is good here. You and your boyfriend should try it some time.'

It was on the tip of Louise's tongue to exclaim, 'He isn't my boyfriend,' but she bit the words back. After all, it didn't matter in the least what Anna thought. Or Mark either.

Colin was waiting for her by the door and she said a quick goodbye and went to join him.

He smiled and slipped his arm round her and, thus linked, they left the pub and walked to the car.

It was inevitable that he should kiss her when he put her down at the station and Louise accepted it as the normal ending to such an evening. But as she cycled home through the dusk she was uneasy. It wouldn't do to get too involved with Colin, much as she liked him, and it might not be very easy to avoid it while he was constantly visiting his brother.

But for a time her foreboding seemed without foundation, although it was largely due to pure chance. The next time he came to Sinclair ward she was very busy with an operation case which required constant monitoring. She saw nothing of Colin except a backview as she passed. Then his visit coincided with her day off, and the next day Robert told her Colin wouldn't be coming again because he would be away for two weeks on holiday.

'I shall miss him,' he said. 'He always cheers me up.'

'But you're much stronger now,' Louise pointed out gently. 'You don't need him so much.'

It was true that he was progressing. He was getting over the physical shock of his operation and even his mental condition was not so depressed as it had been.

A brightly coloured postcard came from Colin, sent from Torremolinos, saying *Wish you were here. We must get together again when I'm back.* Louise read it without any feeling of envy and tossed it into the wastepaper basket. He probably didn't really mean it.

From a nursing point of view her life seemed to have settled into an orderly pattern, even if it tended to be rather breathless. She rode her bicycle to the station, sat briefly in the train and got out at the big bustling station in Marchester. From there she rapidly walked the half-mile to the hospital and began the day's work.

When it was her day off she lazed at home or wandered on the marshes, according to the weather or the state of the tide. Once or twice she passed Creek House but she saw no sign of life. The grass, she noted, badly needed cutting.

And then, one day, the pattern changed.

Louise had wondered several times about the other nurse from her agency, Celia Browning. She had looked out for her in the canteen but Marchester General had hundreds of nurses and there were many who, for one reason or another, wore the uniform of a different hospital. Any of them could be Celia. Twice she had made tentative enquiries of a strange nurse without success.

When they did eventually meet it happened completely unexpectedly.

It was a very hot day and Louise had snatched a few minutes during her morning coffee break to wander out into the small rose garden which was all that was left of the once beautifully laid out and well tended grounds.

Another nurse was there already, a small dark girl with a pale skin and an unhappy droop to her lips. Although she wore the blue dress of a staff nurse, it was of a different design and her cap was elaborately pleated. As Louise sat down beside her she heard a stifled sob.

Should she pretend not to have noticed? Maybe that was what the other girl would prefer. Nevertheless Louise decided to risk a snub.

'Is there anything I can do to help?' she asked quitely.

'I shouldn't think so.' There was no sign of resentment in the doleful reply. 'It's my own problem and I've got to face up to it.'

'Sometimes another opinion—'

'Not in this case, but I'd be glad to tell you about it. It might be a relief just to talk. I haven't been able to discuss it with anyone because I'm a stranger.'

'So am I.'

'Are you?' The damp brown eyes widened. 'But you look like the Marchester nurses.'

'That's because I trained here but I've been away for some time. I've only come back temporarily because my agency fixed it. My name's Louise Weston, by the way. What's yours?'

Before she received the answer to her question, she had half guessed what it might be.

'So you're Celia Browning!' she exclaimed. 'We're from the same agency and I've been looking out for you but our paths never seemed to cross. What's the matter, Celia? Don't you like it here?'

'It'd be okay but for one thing—if I hadn't been sent to the children's ward.' She was again on the verge of tears. 'It isn't that I don't like children but I can't *bear* having to nurse them, specially when they're seriously ill. They're so little and pathetic and—and it breaks my heart.'

Although sympathetic, Louise was bewildered. 'Why did you let them send you there? I'm sure if you'd explained—'

'I thought I ought to pull myself together and somehow adjust. It's two years now—' A sob choked her but she swallowed it down and struggled on. 'I lost my own child, you see, when he was three—leukaemia. And it broke up my marriage because my husband had adored him and he just couldn't take it. We got a divorce and I went back to nursing.'

'You look so young and you've got all that behind you!' Louise felt ashamed of her own uneventful existence.

'I'm twenty-six but sometimes I feel forty.'
Celia sighed and paused for a moment. 'Anyway,' she continued, 'I've tried to get used to
nursing children but I just can't. I shall have to
wait a lot longer than two years before I'm
ready for it—if ever.'

'I'm sure if you went to one of the senior
nursing officers and explained the situation
she'd try and get you moved to another ward.'

'I hate causing so much upheaval. It would
be a lot easier if I found someone willing to
change with me.' With an abrupt movement
Celia straightened her drooping shoulders.
'Louise! would *you* change? We're both
agency nurses, only here for a few weeks or
months. If we switched over it wouldn't cause
any upset at all. Which ward are you on?'

'Men's surgical.'

Louise had answered mechanically, her
brief reply giving away nothing of the shock
the suggestion had been to her. And yet why
should she mind? Unlike poor Celia, she had
no reason to dislike nursing children.

The reason for her reluctance was staring
her in the face but she closed her eyes to it.
And it was certainly not one she wanted to put
into words.

'Anderson is a lovely ward,' Celia was
saying eagerly. 'Sister Roberts is super—
young and friendly—and Dr Halliwell couldn't
be nicer. I'm sure you'd be happy there.'

'You like Dr Halliwell?'

There must have been a strange note in Louise's voice for Celia turned her head to glance at her in slight bewilderment.

'I don't know anything about him outside the ward, but in it everybody likes him. *Please* say you'd be willing to change with me if we can get permission.'

CHAPTER SEVEN

IT WAS very quiet in the rose garden, almost the only sound being the hum of distant traffic. A sparrow came and perched on the nearest rose bush, sending some of the scented pink petals fluttering to the ground. But Louise was aware of nothing except the strange feeling that the decision she was being called on to make was of quite extraordinary significance.

'Okay, Celia.' She forced a smile. 'I'll change with you if we can get permission.'

Listening to the girl's fervent thanks, she was deeply ashamed of her own secret hope that permission might be refused. She clung to it right up to the last moment but was not really surprised when the Senior Nursing Officer received their request with sympathetic understanding.

Sister McKinley was not at all pleased. She had quickly learnt to appreciate a staff nurse who had rapidly adapted to the routine of her ward. But Sister Roberts welcomed Louise to the children's ward with cheerful good humour.

'I'm sure you'll soon settle down in Anderson. What's your Christian name, by the way?

We don't use formal titles here and I shall be
glad if you'll call me Liz.'

She was only a few years older than her new
staff nurse. Her lace-trimmed cap sat jauntily
on a mass of chestnut hair and her bright,
greenish-hazel eyes seemed to be always smiling. She had a well-developed figure which,
moulded by the plain navy blue dress, was
distinctly seductive.

The ward was wide, with cots round the
walls and a play area in the centre. A few
cubicles with sliding glass doors at the top end
were kept for seriously ill children, but otherwise it resembled a large nursery. Primrose
walls and orange curtains gaily decorated with
Magic Roundabout characters made an attractive and sunny background.

After the strict and rather old-fashioned
routine in Sinclair, Louise felt it hard to adapt
to the apparent chaos of Anderson. Mealtimes
were regular and the afternoon rest was insisted on, but otherwise—so it seemed to her—
the children did what they liked. Housemen
came in at all times and played with them, and
parents wandered around, sharing in the work
of nursing.

'When does Dr Halliwell do his round?' she
asked another staff nurse on her first morning.

'We don't have medical rounds in this ward.'
Sarah James pushed back an over-long fringe
of mouse-coloured hair. 'He comes in and out

just like the boys, only he starts a bit later because he lives out in the wilds somewhere and has quite a long drive.'

'Fifteen miles.'

Sarah stared at her. 'Is that all? I thought it was much farther. How do you know?'

'He lives in my village.'

'Really? Why don't you come in together then? I'm sure he wouldn't mind giving you a lift.'

Louise felt herself flushing. 'I wouldn't dream of asking him. Besides, it would be impossible. Our times are completely different.'

'I don't see why he shouldn't take you home sometimes,' Sarah said firmly.

Louise could think of plenty of reasons, the most important being that she would hate it. Besides, she was likely to see as much of Dr Halliwell as she could stand *inside* the ward.

It was quite true, though, that he was different when he was visiting his little patients. That first morning she stared in amazement as she saw him pick up a toy rabbit and waggle its long ears to coax a reluctant smile from an unhappy two-year-old.

So far he didn't know she had been transferred to Anderson, but Liz soon altered that. It was apparently her habit to give him coffee in the office when he had checked on the children's progress, and she called Louise in to be introduced.

'This is Louise Weston, Mark. She's come to join the Anderson nurses and I think she's finding it a bit bewildering.' The brilliant smile flashed out, including the new staff nurse in its warmth.

'Louise and I have already met.'

Although the words were formal, the tone of voice was pleasantly friendly and Louise had to restrain herself from showing her amazement. Liz Roberts must have a remarkably good influence on him.

'We live near each other,' Mark continued, and went on to talk about Vicky's illness.

'You told me you'd found somebody to look after your little girl but I never guessed it might have been our new nurse. That was a lucky break, wasn't it?'

'Very lucky,' he said evenly.

So far Louise had not managed to get in a word. She felt awkward, standing there in silence, and the polite smile which she had conjured up had quickly faded. Snatching the first opportunity of saying something, she asked after Anna.

'She's much more mobile than she was,' Mark told her. 'She even contrives to get up and down the stairs now and that makes a lot of difference. I'm afraid it means considerable effort for her but she doesn't give in easily.'

'So I've always understood,' Liz put in smoothly.

The sister's expression had scarcely altered but Louise thought she detected a slight change in the atmosphere, a discordant note which hadn't been there before Anna's name was mentioned. Puzzled, she asked permission to leave the ward for her coffee break.

'Yes, of course,' Liz said. 'I'd offer you some here but it's good for you nurses to get away from this bedlam for a little while.'

After that, Louise inevitably saw a good deal of the paediatrician and she gradually learnt to accept the change in him and to associate it entirely with the ward. Once, when Sister was off duty, she was obliged to walk round with him and she marvelled afresh at his sure touch with the children.

What a pity that he couldn't treat his own child the same way! He shouldn't still have been feeling so bitter about the circumstances of her birth, but that showed the sort of person he was. Quite clearly the kind, good-tempered Dr Halliwell known to Anderson ward was only a façade. The real man still lurked underneath.

Reaching that conclusion somehow made Louise feel more satisfied about it all. She didn't have to *like* the man just because he was good at his job.

For a time she managed to stand aloof,

taking no part in the general adulation of the children's consultant yet not making it too obvious that she wasn't sharing in it. And then, one day, her theory about there being two different Dr Halliwells was put to the test.

They had been exceptionally busy in the early evening due to an outbreak of mild food poisoning after a birthday party. None of the children was seriously ill, but having to admit eight of them had strained the resources of the ward to the utmost. Consequently Louise missed her usual train home and had to depart at speed to have any hope of catching the next.

She was racing past the staff car park when a low red car shot out and passed her, only to brake violently and stop. The driver's window was wide open and Mark leaned out.

'Want a lift?'

From one point of view it was the last thing Louise wanted, but she couldn't help thinking wistfully of how much more quickly she would get home if she accepted. Besides, it would be unnecessarily rude to refuse.

'Thanks.' Increasing her speed still further, she caught him up and jumped in.

'We really ought to do this more often,' Mark said as they joined the traffic streaming past the hospital.

Stealing a glance at his face Louise discovered that he was half smiling. He was still the Dr Halliwell of Anderson ward—pleasant, friendly and obviously happy to do a good turn. It would be interesting to discover when the change occurred. Half-way home perhaps?

'It wouldn't be practicable, since we rarely leave at the same time,' she pointed out. 'I expect your times vary a lot, but mine are supposed to be regular.'

'I'm afraid you're very late today, but it couldn't be helped.'

'Oh no, of course it couldn't. I wasn't complaining—just stating a fact.' She turned towards him impulsively. 'Those poor little children—what a shame that a party should end like that. Do you think somebody has been careless?'

'Most certainly *somebody* has, but I should think it's very unlikely to be the birthday child's mother. She didn't strike me as being the type to take risks with food.'

The subject lasted them until they turned off the ring road and headed towards Deenham Market. Then a silence fell which Louise found impossible to break.

It was Mark who finally put an end to it.

'How do you like being back in a general hospital?' he asked. 'It must be very different from private nursing.'

'It makes a welcome change, and I like living at home again. I don't mind the train journey at all.'

'People thought I was crazy when I moved

o it to Barkington but it's worked out very well.' His voice changed and he was suddenly much more the Mark whom Louise thought she knew. 'I was thankful to get away from the social side of hospital life, the parties and gossip, and the feeling of living in a goldfish bowl. I think a doctor's private life should *be* private.'

What exactly had the grapevine said about him? Louise wondered, not for the first time. Everybody would know about Anna joining the household and it would be bound to cause comment.

'You get a lot of gossip in villages too,' she pointed out.

'Really?' He sounded surprised. 'Not that it matters anyway. At Creek House we're well out of it and people can say what they like.'

They came to Deenham Market and drove on another mile to Barkington. As she got out at Holly Lodge Louise reverted to their previous conversation.

'I hope the food poisoning cases are all better tomorrow. It's my day off so I may not see any of them again.'

'Most of them will be discharged quite soon.' Mark looked up at her, a strange expression on his face. 'Enjoy your day, Louise. I'm sure you deserve it.'

She stared after him as he drove off down the road, bewildered by what he had said. It was ordinary enough and probably meant nothing, but it wasn't like him. He had scarcely reverted at all to the Mark Halliwell she had previously known and her theory about his dual personality had not stood up very well to the test.

Shrugging the problem away, she entered the garden, and at that moment her mother appeared out of the dusk on her way to the compost heap with a barrow full of weeds.

'You're very late tonight, dear, and where's your bicycle?'

'I'm sure you can't possibly see to do any gardening,' Louise exclaimed. 'It'll be dark soon and you'll be pulling up plants instead of weeds.'

'The evenings are certainly drawing in. Mrs Taunton mentioned it only this morning. What have you done with your bicycle?'

'It's still at the station. I was late and got a lift home with Dr Halliwell.' Louise went hurrying on. 'I can walk to Deenham and fetch it tomorrow.'

It was a chore which remained at the back of her mind for most of her free day. Rain was threatening and she felt reluctant to undertake a mile-long walk which might include getting caught in a downpour. Consequently she pottered about the house all morning, finding plenty to do and yet aware all the time of a strange restlessness. In the afternoon it really

did rain, but by early evening the clouds had
rolled away and a misty sun was turning the
marshes to shining bronze.

'If you put off fetching your bicycle much
longer,' her mother reminded her impatiently,
'it will still be at the station when you need it in
the morning.'

'I'll go now,' Louise said with sudden decision.

She enjoyed the walk for the air was cool
and she didn't mind the strong smell of seaweed and mud as the tide went down, leaving
vast stretches of the marshes uncovered. But
the exercise did nothing to dispel that odd,
restless feeling, and half-way home she was
seized by an impulse which caused her to turn
down one of the rough tracks which, a little
above water level except in times of flood, led
towards the distant sea.

Cars came this way at weekends and during
the school holidays, but this evening it was
deserted and the only sound was the sighing of
the wind in the reeds and the harsh cries of sea
birds feeding on the shoreline. There was a
yellow, eerie light which a stranger might have
found frightening, but Louise had seen it many
times before and she cycled on regardless.

After a while she bumped her way to the
beach, where tiny waves lapped ceaselessly on
the sand. The tide was almost at its lowest ebb
and there was a fairly wide stretch on which to

walk. Leaving her bicycle leaning against some tussocks of marsh grass, she turned to the left and began a leisurely stroll along the water's edge.

Looking alternately out to sea or down at her feet when she had to jump over tiny streamlets, Louise felt herself slowly relaxing as the lonely beauty all around gently soothed her restlessness. Consequently the shock was all the greater when she glanced up and found she wasn't alone after all.

Mark stood there, his dark figure outlined against the silver of sea and sky. He, too, was staring out to sea, but as he became aware of Louise's approach he turned his head to look at her.

Her heart gave a sudden lurch. If it had been possible she would have swung round and fled, but to do so would have been absurd. She had no alternative but to walk on until she reached him.

His opening remark was conventional. 'A lovely evening after the rain.'

'Yes.' Louise moistened her lips but could think of nothing to add.

'I've never been as far as this before,' Mark went on conversationally. 'In fact, I hadn't realised there was a beach here at all.'

'This end of it is only approachable at low tide, and the walk to it from Creek House can be dangerous.'

'I came along the bank. It seemed okay to me.'

'But I expect you had to jump several channels flowing into the creek?'

'Well, yes, a few.' He exhibited muddy shoes. 'They were no problem at all.'

The last time they had discussed the marshes he had seemed to be well aware of the dangers and Louise was exasperated because his increased knowledge of them appeared to have made him careless.

'Those channels will get rapidly wider when the tide starts coming in,' she insisted. 'You'll have to watch it going back. It's a very long walk round by the way I came.'

'Then you'd better return by my route.' He smiled. 'So you can make sure I don't do something daft.'

'I can't. I've got my bicycle waiting for me.'

'That bike of yours! It dominates your life, doesn't it? It always seems to be in the wrong place.'

'I don't know what I'd do without it,' Louise said aggressively, 'and to my mind it's not in the wrong place at the moment. I never thought of going back along the creek.'

'Don't let's argue about it.' His voice was quiet and peaceable. 'Let's just stand here and enjoy all this incredible beauty. Until I came to Creek House I never understood that flat muddy places like salt marshes could be so attractive.'

'They've always been my favourite place of retreat,' Louise said dreamily. 'As soon as I was old enough to come here alone I began to use the marshes as a sort of—of release. When you're all tensed up and bothered about something, you begin to feel better as soon as you escape by yourself to a lonely spot like this.'

'By yourself?' he asked softly. 'You think solitude is essential?'

'Well, yes—it always seemed so.'

'I'm not sure I agree with that.'

They had been standing very close and with a sudden movement Mark came nearer still and slipped his arm round her shoulders. She stood rigidly, willing herself not to tremble, as she struggled to subdue the pounding of her heart.

What was the matter with her? Why did she feel this overwhelming magnetism, this strange sensation of weakness and rapture? A short time ago she would have said Mark was the last person with whom she wished to share her secret retreat, but now she knew with a terrible clarity that everything had changed. To be here with him was a crazy happiness which she had never before experienced.

'Louise—' His voice was low and husky as he gently turned her to face him. 'I think there must be magic in the air tonight—midsummer madness, perhaps.'

'Midsummer's long past,' she managed to say.

'Perhaps it lingers on in these strange wild places—but never mind that. We don't really need any excuse, do we?'

The gentleness vanished as he took her in his arms. With a primitive savagery he captured her lips and forced them apart, and Louise responded with a passion almost equal to his. Sea and sky swam before her eyes and she closed them to shut out everything except the intoxication of the moment.

How long it lasted she had no idea, but when they at last drew apart, breathing hard, it seemed that even the outside world had changed. A small sickle moon had appeared in the darkening sky and the wash of the sea had become urgent.

'You must go,' Louise said shakily, 'or you won't get back safely.'

Mark looked down at her, his eyes glinting in what remained of the daylight. 'What a practical mind you have! From magic to mud in one easy lesson.'

She was unhappily aware that the magic was receding fast and her reply was as swift and deadly as the thrust of a dagger.

'You're far too important a person to take risks. What would they do in Anderson if you got drowned on the marshes? They've put you on a pedestal there—the whole lot of them.'

Seeing his astonished expression at the sudden onslaught, she hurried on. 'I don't suppose Vicky'd be all that much upset, since you admit you're not a very good father to her, but what about Anna? *She* would miss you terribly—'

'For God's sake,' Mark almost shouted, 'what's got into you, Louise? You enjoyed what's just happened as much as I did. Why do you have to go on like this? Why can't you just take it in your stride?'

She could have given him his answer in a few words, but instead she turned and ran back along the beach, stumbling over stones and splashing through the tiny streams regardless of wet feet. For the first time in her life she was going to return from the marshes in a worse frame of mind than when she had entered them.

The words which had been left unsaid still hammered in her brain and she whispered them softly to the mudflats and the sea. 'Oh, Mark—I think I'm in love with you.'

CHAPTER EIGHT

PEDALLING furiously, Louise rode home as though pursued by the evil black dog which some of the older villagers believed to inhabit the marshes. She arrived scarlet and gasping, and shut herself in the bathroom for a prolonged session with shampoo and bubbles, which seemed the only way of escaping her mother's observant eye.

Sanity returned slowly. By morning she had succeeded in convincing herself that of course she wasn't in love with Mark. Some mysterious outside force must have taken possession of her during that scene on the beach. Maybe it had possessed him too, as he had suggested, but that seemed unlikely.

It was much more probable that he was accustomed to making the most of his opportunities where the feminine sex was concerned.

She had for some time suspected that Sister was a little in love with him. Liz had a way of looking at him with her head very slightly on one side which was definitely provocative. Perhaps there had been gossip about them and that was one reason why he'd been so anxious to escape from Marchester? Driven by an inner compulsion, Louise resolved to find out.

In the meantime she had to meet Mark in the ward and behave as though nothing had happened. She dreaded it all the way to the hospital, but when they did actually encounter each other he was so entirely free from embarrassment that Louise found it quite easy too.

She was in one of the cubicles when he appeared, sponging a little boy with a mysterious and alarmingly high temperature. Sister was with him and they examined the chart together, their heads very close. He had given Louise a nod of greeting, which she acknowledged with a quiet and formal, 'Good-morning, Doctor.'

She stood back as he made a brief examination and then continued with her work. As she gently dried the small, hot body she felt more than ever certain that it had been nothing but opportunism which had inspired last night's incident.

But she still felt that urgent need to discover more about Mark's love life, and when she and Sarah James left the ward together at lunchtime she deliberately manoeuvred the conversation in that direction.

'Have you nursed in Anderson long?' she asked when they were seated at a small table in the canteen.

'Ever since I became a staff nurse and that's

nearly two years. I don't want to nurse anywhere else. It's not just that I like children but
the ward is such a happy one.'

'Largely due to Liz, I suppose,' Louise said
thoughtfully.

'Oh yes. If she suddenly decided to leave, I
might have to think twice about staying on
myself.'

'She's very attractive. Surely there must be a
man in her life?'

'If there is she's been remarkably clever in
keeping it to herself.' Sarah balanced a piece
of lettuce on her fork. 'The only man I've
ever heard her name linked with is Mark
Halliwell.'

Louise bent her head over her plate and
kept her eyes veiled to hide her sudden interest. Schooling her voice to sound as casual
as possible, she asked whether they had had an
affair.

'Not as far as is generally known, but he
took her out sometimes because various people have seen them at the theatre or a res-
taurant. Not recently though.'

'Why would that be?' Louise asked innocently.

'Well, I suppose it dates from the arrival of
that new housekeeper. She was the one who
really got the grapevine humming.'

'Having met Anna, I can imagine that.'

'I think he was a bit silly to import such a

young and attractive girl into his household—
foreign too, and that always seems more sug-
gestive, though I'm sure I don't know why it
should.' Sarah leaned forward and lowered
her voice. 'I believe Liz still likes him.'

'It was because I sort of sensed something in
the way she looks at him that I asked you,'
Louise confessed.

'So you've noticed it too? Poor Liz—she
must hate to think of that Danish girl living
with him.' Sarah broke off abruptly and
laughed. 'I didn't mean that exactly, though it
may be the case for all I know.'

Louise remembered the connecting door
between the two front rooms at Creek House.
It was hard to believe that it was never made
use of. And suddenly she wished fervently that
she had never embarked on this conversation.

'After getting himself talked about in hospital circles,' Sarah was saying, 'you'd think
he'd have more sense than to move to a village.
The local people must think the situation a bit
odd.'

'I rarely hear gossip so I wouldn't know. My
personal friends, I'm sure, couldn't care less
about what goes on at Creek House. It's a very
isolated place and anybody living there can
have quite a secret life.'

What would Sarah think if she knew about
last night? Louise wondered as she finished her
lunch. Perhaps she wouldn't be surprised. It

certainly seemed that Mark had built himself up quite a reputation for womanising.

One thing was for sure. He wouldn't get another opportunity where Louise was concerned. And as for imagining herself to be in love with him, she must have been out of her mind.

It was definitely as a result of her enquiries regarding Mark and her inward disgust at the way she had allowed herself to be swept off her feet that, the next time she met Colin, she greeted him with rather more than a friendly warmth.

'How's your brother getting on?' she asked as they stood talking in the hospital grounds at the start of the evening visiting hour.

His face, which had brightened at the sight of her, lengthened into lines of gloom. 'Not too good. I believe he's pretty sure what's the matter with him but is afraid to ask outright. He's definitely got something on his mind.'

'That often happens with cancer patients. They seem to develop a sort of sixth sense about themselves. But, on the other hand, people sometimes imagine they've got cancer when there's nothing seriously wrong with them at all.'

Colin was not really listening. He was running his fingers up and down her arm in an absent way, as thought turning something over in his mind. Eventually he said abruptly, 'Have you got a train to catch?'

'Yes, of course.' She glanced at her watch. 'I ought to be on my way.'

'Come up to the ward with me. It'll be a change for Rob to see somebody different, and then I'll run you home after the visit.'

Louise hesitated only momentarily and then agreed to do as Colin had suggested. After the playroom atmosphere of Anderson the surgical ward seemed abnormally quiet in spite of the little groups of visitors. Robert Mason had been moved since she saw him last, but was still near the upper end of the ward. He greeted them listlessly but managed to produce a wan smile for Louise.

As they sat down side by side, Celia Browning came past carrying a big bunch of sweet peas and paused to greet them.

'How are you liking it here?' Louise asked her.

The girl's naturally pale face lighted up at once. 'Immensely, thanks. I can really get my teeth into this sort of nursing. I shall always be grateful to you for changing with me.'

'Is that why you disappeared to the children's ward?' Colin asked in surprise as Celia hurried on her way. 'I assumed you were moved by the powers that be for a reason nobody else could guess.'

'That certainly seems to happen sometimes,

but there was a good reason on this occasion.'
Louise hesitated and then decided to tell him
what it was.

He listened with more interest than she had
expected. 'So that's why that little nurse looks
the way she does. I sort of sensed life hadn't
treated her very well the first time I saw her.'

'She's a lovely nurse,' Robert said unexpectedly. 'Really makes you feel you matter to
her, and that's more than you can say for
some.'

'I'm sure you matter to every single one of
them,' Louise told him firmly. 'It's just that
some aren't so good at showing it without
getting themselves too involved. It's not easy
to strike just the right attitude.'

They stayed until the bell was rung, talking
quietly but getting very little response from the
patient. As they left the ward Colin gave a long
sigh.

'You see what I mean? He's so kind of—
unapproachable.'

'I expect he still feels low after the operation. It takes ages.'

His face darkened. 'Don't hand out that
bromide to me, Louise, *please*. I thought we
were friends.'

'Sorry.' She was genuinely regretful. 'I'm
afraid it gets to be a habit, and with some
people it's what they want to hear.'

'You nurses always tell people what you

think they want to hear?' he demanded.

'No, of course not,' Louise exclaimed a little sharply.

Colin slipped his arm through hers. 'I'm in a filthy mood tonight—thoroughly fed up and depressed. I'm hoping that you'll cheer me up on the drive to Deenham.'

Feeling sorry for him—he was obviously very fond of his brother—Louise did her best. When they said good-night at the station she allowed him a rather warmer embrace than an ordinary farewell justified. Riding her bicycle home afterwards she wondered if it mightn't have been a mistake. She didn't want to get involved with Colin. Or anyone else.

Nevertheless, when he invited her to see a film with him a few days later, she could think of no way of refusing without hurting him. Her mother was glad she had had an invitation from an old friend and could not think why she was so unenthusiastic about accepting it.

'I remember Colin Mason. He always seemed to be a nice boy and you got on very well with him.' Marion hesitated for a moment, watching Louise as she ironed a summer dress. 'He'd do nicely for you to invite to the October Ball,' she suggested with a casualness which did not deceive her daughter.

'The what?' Louise asked with deliberate vagueness.

Marion flung her an exasperated glance. 'I'm talking about the October Ball, so don't sound as though you've never heard of it. It's still the big event of the hospital year, I believe, and you used to look forward to it when you were a student nurse. They still hold it, don't they?'

'Oh yes. There are plenty of posters about it on the notice-boards around the hospital, but it's not yet, Mum. We're only at the end of August and, by tradition, the ball is always on October 1st, unless it's a Sunday. There's lots of time.' She frowned at a crease which had mysteriously appeared. 'And anyway, I'm not at all sure I want to ask Colin.'

'Well, it's your affair, of course, but don't leave it too late in case somebody else snaps him up. He's probably got to know several nurses through visiting his brother so regularly.'

'It wouldn't bother me if he *did* get snapped up,' Louise said crossly. 'I do wish you'd stop trying to pair me off with him.'

Marion sighed. 'I ought to know better at my age. Forget it, dear. If you want to go to the ball no doubt you'll be able to find somebody.'

Louise was not at all sure that she did. In a way it would be fun to dress up and have a glamorous evening out but, on the other hand, she had lost touch with her old friends at the hospital and might find herself and partner isolated among a crowd of strangers.

Consequently, when the other nurses were discussing it, she was non-committal. September began to slip away without any decision being made.

It was Mark who made up her mind for her.

Louise was in charge of the ward one afternoon when he made an unexpected visit. She was sitting in Sister's office, a pleasant room with a big window overlooking the ward, and, busy with some notes, she was taken entirely by surprise.

'Sister off duty?' Mark asked casually, leaning against the doorpost.'

'Yes, but—'

'Doesn't matter. I thought I'd take another look at that child with suspected meningitis. He's still in the first cubicle, I suppose.'

'Yes, Doctor. I'll come with you.'

'There's no need. I know the way, thank you.'

Louise flushed and thought angrily that he was the only man who had the power to make her change colour so frequently. He was very rarely sarcastic when he visited his ward and he must reserve that kind of retort specially for her.

She sat down again and tried to regain the concentration which he had interrupted. Just as she had achieved it he reappeared.

'I still can't make up my mind. The tests were inconclusive but he has so many of the symptoms.'

'I believe it's possible to suffer from a similar illness which isn't so serious, isn't it?' Louise asked.

'Yes, and it's also possible to have meningitis in a mild form.' Mark frowned and sat down on the edge of the desk.

He was so close that Louise could see the fine, dark hairs on the back of his well-shaped hands. The nails were so perfectly manicured, with clear half moons, that they looked professionally tended, though that seemed most unlikely.

Perhaps Anna did them for him?

As the name leapt unbidden into her mind she was astonished to hear it on his lips.

'Anna had the plaster off her ankle yesterday.'

'That's good news.' Louise forced herself to look up with a smile and found his eyes on her face with such intentness that she glanced away hastily. 'How is her walking now?'

'She's very determined and does extremely well, but the ankle is still stiff, naturally. She couldn't possibly dance.'

'Dance?'

'I'm talking about the October Ball,' Mark said impatiently. 'I have to put in an appearance, unfortunately, and if I don't take a partner I shall be fair game for all the elderly consultants' wives who can only do ordinary ballroom dancing but won't admit it. Therefore—' He broke off and stared out at the ward which was, as usual at that time of the day, a confused medley of parents, grandparents and convalescent children.

With fast beating heart Louise waited for him to continue. He was a long time thinking about it and she began to wonder whether, having embarked on a course which obviously required some effort, he was now regretting it.

'It occurred to me,' Mark went on carefully, 'that it might be a good idea if we went to the ball together, since we both live at Barkington. It would simplify getting home afterwards— perhaps even getting there if it should happen to be your day off. Is it?'

Louise gasped and, as he continued to stare at her, hurriedly answered his question. 'I don't know—I haven't thought about it.'

'Well, you'd better find out and then let me know.'

'But—' She made a determined effort to gather her wits together, still not at all sure she wasn't dreaming. 'I haven't said I'll go! I—I'd rather thought of giving the ball a miss.'

'Why?' Mark demanded truculently.

'Well, I'm only temporary at Marchester and I don't know many people and—'

He brushed her excuses aside impatiently. 'You'd be okay with me.'

Louise raised her eyes again and met his cool grey stare. There was a question she needed to ask and she suddenly found the courage to do it.

'Why don't you take Sister instead of me? It really would be much more—suitable.'

'To hell with that!' Mark exploded. 'I don't happen to want to take Liz. It was you I invited—remember?' And with a touch of bitterness he added, 'I don't find your reception of the invitation very flattering.'

'I'm sorry. It—it was kind of you to think of me.'

'Good God—now you've gone to the other extreme.' He jumped off the desk. 'Are you coming or aren't you?'

'Yes, please,' Louise said meekly.

He flung her a suspicious glance, obviously finding her tone as artificial as it had sounded in her own ears, and left the room without another word, banging the door behind him.

Alone, Louise sat idly at the desk, but although her outward appearance was calm, her mind was a seething whirlpool of emotions. Half of her longed to go to the October Ball with Mark, to have the pleasure of his company for the entire evening, and the other half wished equally fervently that he hadn't asked her. His company could so easily turn out to be no pleasure at all but a long battle of conflicting personalities which could only end in pain.

The arrival of an agitated mother with a query concerning her child brought Louise back to the present with a jerk. She dismissed all her difficulties and uncertainties with one sweeping mental gesture and accompanied the mother into the ward. The problem turned out to be a small one, soon solved. But for the rest of that day Mark's astonishing proposition hovered on the fringe of her consciousness, clamouring for attention.

It wasn't until she was in the train on her way home that she allowed herself to dwell on it again. The passage of several hours had done nothing to diminish its surprising nature. *Why* had he chosen to ask her instead of Liz?

And what was the pretty young sister going to say about it? What, in fact, would the other nurses say?

Fortunately Louise managed to keep her invitation to herself for some time. She listened to the others either complaining because they would be on duty, or discussing what they would wear; somehow she managed to dodge any direct questions about her own involvement.

As the days passed it occurred to her that she ought to give some thought to choosing a dress herself.

Owing to the glamorous nature of some of her nursing jobs, she had a good stock of evening dresses in varying lengths. Obviously she would need a long one for the ball and for some reason she felt disinclined to wear any of the three she possessed. The pink was too bright and she was sure Mark wouldn't like it, the green had had wine spilt on it, and the blue—though it was her own favourite—had been worn too often. She would have to buy something new.

Accordingly she visited the shops during a free afternoon and spent an enjoyable couple of hours trying to find a dress which seemed just right. Her eventual choice was a deep, rich cream, cut daringly low in front and with a tight swathed bodice which moulded her firm young breasts to perfection.

'It might have been made for you,' said the sales girl admiringly. 'Have you got a heavy gold necklace to wear with it? It would look just right.'

Louise disagreed. She possessed an amber necklace and matching earrings which had belonged to her grandmother and she thought they would be less obvious than gold.

Well satisfied with her purchase, she left the shop and hurried back to the hospital, where she hid the conspicuous black and yellow bag in her locker. Several people glanced at it when she took it out to go home but no one asked any questions, and for that Louise was thankful. She still hoped to keep the identity of her escort a secret for as long as possible.

Her mind had been so much taken up with Mark's invitation that she had almost forgotten Colin's existence. But that evening he rang up and suggested they should go to the ball together.

'I believe outside people can get tickets if they have hospital staff in their party, so how about you and me making up a party of two, Louise?' He waited for her reply and seemed somehow to sense her dismay. 'Or are you already going to the ball with someone else?'

CHAPTER NINE

COLIN listened quietly to Louise's somewhat laboured explanation.

'I know I've left it rather late,' he admitted when she ground to a halt, 'but I still hoped—well, you know how it is.'

'I don't suppose you've been thinking much about dancing just lately. How is Rob?'

'A bit better, and beginning to talk about going home. That's a good sign, isn't it?'

'It certainly is. That awful apathy was one of the most worrying aspects of his case.'

She was talking as stiltedly as though he'd been a stranger, someone she had only come into contact with because of his relationship with a patient. But this was Colin, whom she'd known for years and once or twice been on the verge of falling in love with.

'That medic who's invited you,' he went on, abruptly reverting to the ball. 'Just how important is he in your life, Louise? That yarn you gave me about only being asked because his regular partner was out of commission sounded phoney to me. I'd much rather you told me the truth. I don't want to pester you when I'm not wanted.'

'Don't be silly! Of course it's true. Why on earth should I make it up? I'm just a substitute and that's all there is to it.'

'So we're still friends?'

'I don't know of any reason why we shouldn't be.'

That seemed to satisfy him, to Louise's relief. For a moment she wished he had rung up earlier, so she could have refused Mark's invitation, but it was a feeling that didn't last, even though she knew she would have enjoyed the evening with Colin.

What her state of mind would be at the end of an evening with Mark she couldn't even begin to guess.

She had been glad on the whole to find that she wouldn't be able to go home to dress on the day of the ball. She would be working nearly up to the last minute.

'Where shall I pick you up?' Mark asked. 'We have to drive to the Town Hall, as I suppose you know, so it had better be somewhere around the hospital.'

'I haven't even worked out where I'm going to change yet.' Louise had a sudden inspiration. 'Don't bother about driving me. I'll get a taxi and meet you at the Town Hall. It's much the simplest way.'

It would also be the least conspicuous, but Louise kept that to herself.

'It sounds a daft arrangement to me,' he

complained. 'Both of us starting out from much the same spot and meeting later on. Why do you want to waste money on a taxi when my car is available?'

'I like to be independent,' Louise said lamely, and was not surprised at his snort of disgust and disbelief.

The day came and her secret was still intact, but she was obliged to take Sarah into her confidence when she begged the loan of her flatlet to change in. The staff nurse, she knew, had a boyfriend who did not care for dancing, and she had offered to work all the evening in order to release someone else.

'Of course you can dress at my place,' Sarah said at once. 'I'll ask the warden to let you in with her master key.' She hesitated and then added carelessly, 'I didn't know you were going. You've been very cagey about it.'

Louise decided on the truth. 'I didn't want everybody to know that Mark Halliwell had asked me.' And she added the explanation she had given Colin.

'How *very* interesting!' Sarah was obviously intrigued. 'I'm sure you don't need me to tell you to watch it. He has quite a reputation, you know.'

'I'm not a student just out of the Nurse Education Centre! I know all about the women in Mark's life and I must admit I'm surprised he asked me instead of Liz.'

'He probably didn't want to get involved with her again. I wonder what his housekeeper thinks about it. I reckon she assumed he'd give the ball a miss this year.'

'He said he was more or less obliged to attend.'

Sarah laughed disbelievingly. 'I can't see him doing anything he didn't want to unless it was for the benefit of his patients. I think he's a super paediatrician but I don't care much for what I've heard about his private life.'

'His private life doesn't bother me.' Louise had had to fight off a strong desire to spring to Mark's defence. 'I'm sure I can take care of myself,' she finished defiantly.

'Famous last words!' Sarah laughed again.

As she got ready that evening, Louise was strangely nervous. Her hands were cold and her cheeks flushed; making up her eyes she was conscious of a slight trembling which seemed to her so ridiculous that she got quite angry with herself. Anyone would think this was her first date . . .

The new dress slipped silkily over her head and settled down over her body as though, as the sales girl had said, it had been made for her. The amber necklace glowed against her tanned skin and she was pleased to note that her lipstick toned perfectly with it. Perhaps it was only due to the make up but it seemed to her that her eyes were unnaturally brilliant, as though lit by some intense inner excitement. Even her hair shone more than usual.

The Town Hall was blazing with light when her taxi deposited her there. A red carpet with a striped canopy overhead led up the steps, but mounting them all alone was something of an ordeal as a number of spectators had gathered to stare and comment.

Louise was glad to reach the comparative seclusion of the foyer. It was crowded with people waiting for friends and she slipped through unnoticed and went to leave her velvet jacket in the cloakroom. A glance in the mirror assured her that her appearance had not suffered during the short drive, and then she could no longer postpone the moment when she must look around for Mark.

There was no sign of him in the foyer. Hovering in the background, she scanned the groups of chattering people in case he had been absorbed into one of them. He was so tall it would have been easy to spot his dark head—if he had been there. But he was neither part of a group nor standing alone. He wasn't visible at all.

Louise waited several minutes and then returned to the cloakroom where she combed her hair and pretended to touch up her lipstick. Eight o'clock he'd said, and it was already nearly twenty minutes past. It was too bad of him to be late.

Returning to her observation post, she looked round hopefully and again drew a blank. As she wondered whether to remain where she was or join the dancing, she heard a familiar voice and swung round to see Andrew Forbes, a stocky, brown-haired young man who was Mark's house physician.

'All alone, Louise? Has he stood you up then?'

For one panic-stricken moment she thought he must be referring to his boss, but then she realised that his question had been a general one. Leaving it unanswered, she gave him a radiant smile.

'Actually I was just going into the ballroom.'

'Me too.' Andrew slipped his arm into hers. 'I've only just arrived. Got hung up because of a new admission which required my skilled attention. I say, this sounds like a snappy number—shall we join in?'

Nearly all the younger people present were on the floor but they pushed their way into a small space and allowed the rhythm to take possession of them. As she danced Louise glanced about her, noting that most of the VIPs were sitting in reserved seats at the end opposite the band, backed by massed pot plants. Mark was not among them, and he didn't seem to be dancing either, though it was hard to be sure in the crush.

Glad of Andrew's company she stayed with

him when the music stopped, talking idly. But when the band began to play again he looked at her ruefully.

'This is a waltz, isn't it? Afraid I'm not much good at that but I'm game to try if you don't mind.'

His summing up of his own ability turned out to be only too correct. Wincing as her toes were trampled on, Louise set her teeth and tried to stick it out. Most of the older guests were dancing now, glad of a tempo which suited them, and among them several younger couples either struggled along, like Louise and her partner, or gave dazzling displays of skill.

Andrew was not very tall and she could see over his shoulder easily. And suddenly she caught a glimpse of Mark. He looked superlative in the severe black and white of a dinner jacket and frilled shirt, a defiantly scarlet bow tie beneath his chin, and he was waltzing with grace, his head bent slightly over his partner.

The girl in his arms was Liz.

Louise felt herself going rigid with shock. So he really *had* stood her up—it was scarcely believable. Her astonishment quickly turned to anger and she burned to tell him what she thought of him.

Andrew was saying something in her ear and she heard herself replying automatically, 'You what?'

'I was only apologising for standing on your

foot—again. Would you rather we sat down?'

On the verge of snatching at the suggestion, Louise hesitated. It would be far better if Mark saw her dancing with Andrew. Then, at least, he would realise she wasn't standing around moping.

Adroitly taking over some of the steering, she managed it so that they passed across Mark's line of vision. Raising her head in an instinctive gesture, she deliberately allowed her eyes to meet his. To her surprise they were blazing with some strong emotion which looked very like fury and he returned her stare with a directness which matched her own.

Andrew stumbled slightly and lost the rhythm, and she said abruptly, 'I think I would like to sit down after all.'

'I don't blame you,' he said humbly, and they made their way to the line of chairs.

The next dance was a modern one with everyone reacting to it as they felt inclined, and Louise and Andrew became separated. As she swayed vigorously to the beat, her eyes half closed, she was suddenly jolted into full awareness when iron fingers closed round her wrist.

It was Mark, his face set and angry. When she instinctively tried to free herself he merely tightened his grip.

'I want a word with you,' he said tersely.

'You're hurting me!'

'It's your own fault if I am.' He glowered down at her. 'Don't you think I've a right to be livid? What the devil do you think you're playing at?'

As Louise gazed at him blankly he began to draw her away from the crowded floor, out into the foyer and into a small room containing chairs and a central table. It was empty, and Mark closed the door and leaned against it, his arms folded.

'Now,' he said, 'I want an explanation.'

'You're not the only one!' Louise had recovered some of her poise. 'I waited for you quite a long time and I don't much care for standing around alone looking like I've been forgotten.'

'It doesn't appeal to me either.'

'I'm quite sure it wouldn't.' She bit her lower lip and got a grip on her temper. 'I think you're the one who's got the explaining to do, so perhaps you'd better start.'

'Very well.' He was standing very straight and looking coldly down his nose at her. 'Perhaps, in spite of all your nursing experience, you didn't know that a doctor can never be sure of keeping an appointment, that he is always liable to get held up by a medical emergency?'

'Is—is that what happened?'

'Clever girl to have guessed so quickly!'

Louise's colour deepened. 'You don't have

to be like that—and you don't seem to have made much attempt to find me when you did eventually turn up. It seems to me that you went straight into the ballroom and started dancing with—with someone else.'

'The foyer was empty. There was no point in doing anything different.'

There was a long pause. As Louise tried to think of something to say her mood changed. Perhaps she had been a little hasty in her judgement? His sarcasm had caught her in a vulnerable spot. She did, of course, know perfectly well that doctors were unreliable where social engagements were concerned.

It was Mark who broke the silence. 'So where do we go from here? Continue on our separate ways or keep to the original arrangement?'

'I—don't mind,' was all she could manage in reply.

'That's flattering, I must say! You'd just as soon spend the evening with Andrew Forbes as with me?'

Louise felt her lips twitching and she allowed the smile to appear. 'He's a nice boy but a rotten dancer and—well, I don't find him very inspiring to talk to.'

'I'm not surprised.' His answering smile was warm and friendly. 'That seems to settle it then. Come along—let's go back to the ballroom.'

The rest of the evening was like a dream
come true. In harmony with her partner and
conscious of looking her best, Louise glowed
with happiness. Mark liked her dress and told
her so, choosing his words with a poetic fancy
which surprised as much as it pleased her.

'That rich cream colour is just like your
personality, and the glow of the amber is your
fiery temper.'

'I haven't got a fiery temper!' she protested,
laughing. 'You're the one who goes in for that
sort of thing.'

'*Me*?' His eyebrows shot up. 'You have to be
joking.'

She was too happy to argue about it and let
the subject drop. At supper he found a table
for two and it somehow seemed as though the
talking, laughing crowd had withdrawn and
left them on their own in their small, private
world.

All too soon it ended and they walked out
into the cool night air for the drive home.

'You're not riding that damn bicycle
tonight, I hope?' Mark asked.

'In this dress? No, thank you. I persuaded
my father to drive me to the station this morning.'

As they left the lighted streets and drove
along an almost empty dual carriageway, an
odd restraint descended on them. They had
talked easily after they made up their quarrel,

exchanging views, discussing their work and
Louise's foreign travel, sometimes laughing
irreverently at their elders; even their silences
had been comfortable.

But now it was different. Searching for
something to say, she wondered uneasily what
had happened to them. Mark was clearly feeling the constraint just as much as she was and
he offered little response to her few attempts
at conversation. Eventually she gave up and
sat quietly in her corner, fighting off a wave of
depression.

It had been a super evening and she
shouldn't be feeling unhappy because it was
over. But even as she pointed that out to
herself, she was aware of the real reason for
her feeling. There would never be another
evening of the same sort. This was the end. She
was, after all, only a substitute.

They drove along Deenham's sleeping main
street and took the Barkington road. Mark
opened the window slightly and the cool wind
from the marshes reached them, bringing with
it the usual seaweed smell.

'It's refreshing after that stuffy Town Hall,'
he said conversationally. 'I hope you're not
feeling a draught?'

'Oh no—I like it.'

'Then let's stop a minute and enjoy it to the
full.'

He was slowing down and Louise's heart

began to beat in great choking thumps. The car stopped in a lay-by and Mark switched off the engine and wound down his window to the bottom.

'As he turned towards her he said quietly, 'You enjoyed the ball?'

'You know I did.'

'So did I.' His arm slid along the back of the seat and he moved nearer. 'An evening like that needs to be rounded off properly—don't you agree?'

'It depends on—on what you mean,' Louise managed to say.

'I mean this.' His mouth was on hers, forcing her head back and his arms held her in a vice.

She could not have escaped if she had wanted to, but that was far from being the case. Her whole body was responding to his and she was as eager to accept his kisses as he was to give them. When he slipped his hand down her cleavage and cupped her breast she shivered with delight and longed with a passionate intensity for total fulfilment.

It was a long time before either of them moved. When Mark at last released her with a sigh, her lips felt bruised and her neck ached, yet even these discomforts were sheer delight to her.

'Hope I haven't spoilt your dress,' he said jerkily.

'It's uncrushable.'

'Just as well.'

'Yes.'

He leaned forward and restarted the engine. 'Better take you home, I suppose. I hope your mother isn't the sort of woman who sits up?'

'Goodness, no! She had a tendency that way when I was a teenager but I got her out of it long ago.'

Exactly why she introduced the subject of Anna, Louise never knew. It came into her head and was spoken before she could stop it.

'Will Anna be listening for your return?'

The atmosphere changed immediately. Mark glanced at her and his reply was curt.

'I sincerely hope not. The ball ended at midnight and it's now two o'clock. She might—er—think there'd been an accident.'

'I suppose that would worry her quite a lot.'

'Naturally.' He stopped outside Holly Lodge. 'Good-night, Louise—thank you for coming.

'Thank you for taking me,' she said politely.

She did not expect him to kiss her again and he made no move to do so. Letting herself into the house as silently as possible she wondered bitterly what in the world had made her ask that stupid question about Anna. It had introduced a jarring note and spoilt everything.

Everything? No, of course not. Apart from its unfortunate beginning, the evening had been a huge success and she would remember it always. Except the interlude in the lay-by. That had better be forgotten as soon as possible since it had, as Mark himself had said, merely 'rounded off the evening.'

CHAPTER TEN

SOMEONE was shaking her. Louise made a small sound of protest and turned over in bed.

'Wake up!' It was her mother's voice. 'What on earth are you thinking of this morning? Didn't you hear the alarm?'

'Alarm?' Louise forced her eyes wide open. 'Has it gone then?'

'I don't know, dear, but it's certainly getting very late. Do try and pull yourself together.'

'Did I set it last night? I can't remember doing so.' She stared blearily at the clock and leapt out of bed. 'I've just got to catch that train.'

'You *must* have enjoyed yourself if you forgot about the alarm! Shall I bring your breakfast up so you can eat while you dress?'

'I haven't got time to eat—just a mug of coffee, please, Mum.' Louise searched frantically for clean underwear and dived for the bathroom.

Never had the ride to Deenham seemed so long. She pedalled furiously but she was still only just within sight of the church spire when the toot of a diesel engine told her she had lost the race with the clock.

There wouldn't be another train for nearly an hour.

To be late on the morning after the Hospital Ball was terribly bad timing. Only too well aware of the reason for forgetting to set the alarm and angry with herself because of it, Louise paced up and down the platform until the regular exercise began to induce a calmer frame of mind.

It was done now and she would have to face up to the amused and curious comments of her friends at the hospital as best she could. Reaching the ward at last she went straight to Sister to apologise.

Liz gave her a long, level stare, her mouth unsmiling. 'You're very late, Nurse,' she said curtly before Louise could speak.

To be called 'Nurse' instead of by her Christian name was a sure sign that Liz was in a bad mood. Such moods were rare and consequently had a greater impact.

Louise told the exact truth. 'I'm sorry, Sister. I somehow forgot to set the alarm, and by the time my mother realised I wasn't getting up it was too late to catch my usual train.'

'It's the first time you've missed it.' Sister's tone had changed slightly and become more friendly. 'I suppose I shouldn't take too much notice of it, specially in these days when discipline is so lax.' She paused, her slightly plump fingers playing with a pen lying on the desk.

'But there is something I must say to you which you may consider an unwarranted interference in your private life. However, I intend to take a chance and get it off my mind.'

Louise stared at her in surprise, for the moment unable to guess what might be coming. She was not left long in doubt.

'It was impossible not to notice last night that you were spending the evening with Dr Halliwell. He is, of course, a very attractive man and a wonderful children's doctor, but unfortunately his reputation isn't all it might be. I thought, since you're a newcomer to the hospital, you might not be aware of that.'

The hot colour which had blazed in Louise's cheeks drained away, leaving her rather white. With head held high she thrust back at Liz.

'You were quite right when you said it was unwarranted interference! Do you think you're talking to an inexperienced student nurse? I've been around, you know—probably more than you have. As for Dr Halliwell's reputation, I know all about it, thank you.'

'I'm sorry,' Liz said stiffly. 'I meant well.'

'I also know,' Louise rushed on, 'that it was ill-natured gossip—and nothing else—which made him leave Marchester to go and live at Creek House, well away from everybody.'

'He asked for it, getting that Danish girl to be his housekeeper. People were bound to talk.'

At the mention of Anna, desolation abruptly swept over Louise, robbing her of the anger which had sustained her. It was probably all true, what *they* said about Mark. He had gone around with Liz and then imported Anna into his home and switched his attentions to her. And now he was making it very plain that he found her—Louise—attractive.

No doubt when his 'housekeeper' was fully recovered he would forget all about the nurse who had temporarily interested him.

'Yes,' she agreed dully, 'people would be unlikely to let an opportunity like that slip.'

Liz sighed, and for a moment an odd bond of sympathy united them. Then the sister made a gesture of dismissal.

'You'd better get on with your work. We're extremely busy this morning and that emergency who was admitted last night is very poorly.'

The emergency turned out to be a burns case. A little girl of three had pulled a saucepan of boiling water off the cooker and over a large part of her body. She was in one of the cubicles, moaning softly to herself and with a distracted mother in attendance.

'I never thought she'd touch it, Nurse.' A strained white face with desperate eyes turned towards Louise. 'She's always been sensible about that sort of thing. Will she be dreadfully marked?'

'It's too early to answer that question.' Although she was desperately sorry for both of them, Louise knew the mother was to blame. 'At present we're more concerned with the shock she's had. She's going to need a lot of care.'

Behind her she sensed that someone had entered the cubicle, but until Mark spoke she had assumed it was another nurse. The sound of his voice sent her pulses racing even at such a moment and she withdrew hastily, leaving him to answer the mother's questions.

He had given her one brief glance, his face inscrutable. She had no means of judging whether he was thinking of last night or whether he had already relegated it to the cluttered corner of his mind where he kept similar recollections.

'So you've got here then?' It was Sarah, pausing on her way to the bathroom with two convalescent toddlers. 'What happened?'

As patiently as possible Louise explained.

'I warned you, didn't I?' Sarah quite plainly considered it funny. 'That man has a devastating effect on women—though not on me, I'm glad to say. Was Liz very angry with you?'

'Fairly, but I don't suppose she'll hold it against me.'

'Shouldn't think so.' Sarah began to move away. 'I must say you were an idiot to forget to set your alarm. It must have been some evening!'

She was half laughing as she spoke and her voice had been clearly audible. As Louise turned in the opposite direction she found Mark at her side.

'I couldn't help overhearing,' he said curtly. 'Did you miss your train this morning?' And when she confirmed it he demanded incredulously, 'Why on earth didn't you ring me and ask for a lift?'

'I—I didn't think of it.'

'I can't imagine why not. It seems to me the obvious solution.'

In some cases it might have been the natural thing to do, Louise admitted as he went away down the ward. But this wasn't a normal situation and, in a sudden flight of fancy, she saw herself as a moth struggling against a fatal magnetism which could bring nothing but unhappiness. Her only hope lay in doing all in her power to avoid any contact with Mark outside the hospital.

It should have been easy, but in actual fact it turned out to be extraordinarily difficult.

Her next day off coincided with one of her mother's jam-making days. It was blackberry and apple this time and the kitchen was full of the rich smell of boiling fruit when Marion gave an exclamation of annoyance.

'I forgot to stock up with jam pot covers

yesterday when I was in the shop. Would you mind, dear?'

So Louise got out her bicycle and pedalled off in the direction of the village stores. On the way she had to pass the house where Janet Mayhew, a friend of her mother's, held her play school. It was twelve o'clock and the children were coming out and being picked up by waiting mothers. Out of the corner of her eye she thought she spotted Vicky standing just inside the gate.

When she returned with the covers the child was at the edge of the road, and Mrs Mayhew with her. As she passed the teacher called out to her.

'Did you happen to see a car coming along the creek road when you passed the end of it?'

'I didn't notice.' Louise put on her brakes and jumped off. She said, 'Hello, Vicky,' and received a shy smile in return.

'It's too tiresome. I've got a lunch date in Marchester and I simply must catch the twelve-forty-five train because I'm meeting a friend and we're going to the theatre this afternoon, but this child hasn't been collected. Anna is a bit unreliable time-wise but she's never been really late. I can't think what's happened to her.'

'The car was ever so hard to start this morning,' Vicky volunteered. 'I expect it's got something wrong with its inside.'

'I sincerely hope not—' Mrs Mayhew broke off and hurried away to answer the telephone which was ringing in the hall.

She was back within seconds looking more annoyed than before.'

'That wretched Danish girl! She's just phoned from Marchester, if you please, to say the car's let her down completely and will I keep Vicky until this evening! She rang off before I had a chance to explain that it was impossible. Now what am I going to do?'

It seemed so natural to offer to help that Louise made her suggestion without stopping to think.

'Don't worry, Mrs Mayhew. I'll look after Vicky. We know each other quite well because I nursed her when she was ill.'

'Oh, thank you—you are kind!' The child was handed over with obvious relief. 'Be a good girl, Vicky. I expect you'll be able to go home soon.'

Pushing her bicycle along the road and listening to the little girl's chatter, Louise was suddenly struck by an unwelcome thought. The arrangement had been made in such a hurry that she had overlooked the existence of what should have been a self-evident difficulty.

No one would know where Vicky was.

Anna was out of reach in Marchester, presumably waiting for the car to be repaired, but she would doubtless turn up eventually at the play school, to find it locked up and no sign of either the teacher or Mark's little girl. She would certainly be worried and, although Louise couldn't manage to feel unduly distressed because of it, she would have preferred to let the housekeeper know.

It was her mother who suggested a solution.

'Why don't you phone Dr Halliwell at the hospital? If Anna has contacted him about the car he may know where to find her. It's worth a try.'

'Do you really think so?' Louise said doubtfully.

'Of course I do. Go and do it now, dear, while Vicky helps me cover the jam.'

So Louise went reluctantly to the telephone.

'I don't know where he is just now,' said the voice on the switchboard. 'Is it important?'

'Well, it is actually. Would you bleep him, please?'

There was a considerable pause and then Mark's voice barked in her ear. 'Dr Halliwell here.'

Willing herself to speak coolly and calmly, Louise began, 'I thought you ought to know that I've got Vicky with me.'

'*You* have? But Anna said she'd asked Mrs Mayhew to keep her.'

'It wasn't possible, and Anna didn't give her a chance to explain.'

'I don't suppose it occurred to her that there
would be any difficulty. I don't quite understand how you got involved but it doesn't
matter. One of us will pick Vicky up, but it
won't be very early, even if Anna comes,
because the car won't be ready until six
o'clock. Will that be okay?'

'Oh yes, thank you. My mother and I don't
mind looking after her in the least.'

'It's very good of you,' Mark said form-
ally.

As Louise replaced the receiver she was
obliged to struggle with ridiculous tears. She
wanted so very much more from him than this
cool politeness; even his bad temper would
have been preferable. It was almost impossible
to believe that he had held her in his arms and
kissed her so passionately only a few nights
ago.

It was a few minutes before she regained her
composure sufficiently to report back to her
mother.

'I knew it was a good idea to ring him,'
Marion said complacently.

She unearthed a box of old toys and, since
the weather was warm for October, Vicky
played with them in the garden. About half-
past five a car stopped at the gate.

'It looks as though your Daddy's come to
fetch you,' Louise said uneasily.

'I'm not ready to go! I haven't finished play-

ing with these toys yet.' Vicky turned her back
as Mark came up the drive.

'You've got plenty of your own at home,' he
said impatiently.

'But these are different. They're much more
int'resting.'

'Come on, dear,' Marion said firmly,
appearing suddenly. 'Daddy won't want to be
kept waiting. I expect he's had a busy day.'

Louise stole a glance at Mark and immediately saw that he was having difficulty in
controlling his exasperation. No doubt her
mother was right when she said he'd had a busy
day and he would be anxious to get back to the
peace and quiet of Creek House.

Vicky stood up reluctantly and then suddenly ran to Louise and clung to her. 'I want to
show Louise my new dolls' house. Can't she
come back with us?' She raised her big eyes
beseechingly.

'Certainly,' he said at once, 'but I don't
think she'll want to bother.'

'You *will* want to bother, won't you?' Vicky
begged.

'Perhaps I'll come another time,' Louise
suggested gently.

'No! I want you to come now.'

Marion glanced from Mark to her daughter
in a puzzled way, as though wondering why
they both sounded so uptight. She had made
very little comment when Louise went to the

ball with him—for which Louise was exceedingly grateful—but it was clear that her natural curiosity regarding their relationship, if any, was bubbling beneath the surface.

'It might be a good idea to avoid tears,' she now said quietly. 'The child's a bit overtired perhaps. I think you should go, Louise.'

'You wouldn't have to walk back,' Mark said. 'I'll drive you as soon as Anna gets there.'

To be alone with him in the car—it was the last thing she wanted, yet she could see no way of avoiding it without making an unnecessary fuss.

'All right, I'll come.' She smiled down at Vicky and went to fetch her anorak.

No one spoke during the short drive. The marshes were already misty after the warm day and Creek House loomed up darkly with a slightly sinister air.

Vicky was the first to enter and she went racing up the stairs, calling out to Louise to follow her. The dolls' house was in her room, a magnificent affair in mock-Tudor style.

'It's beautiful.' Louise knelt down to peer inside. 'Have you had a birthday?'

'My birthday's in March. Daddy gave me this because I'd been such a good girl and helped Anna when she couldn't walk properly.'

'I see,' Louise said flatly.

Mark was calling from downstairs, suggesting a drink, and she hesitated, looking at the child.

'Are you coming down, love?'

'No, thank you. I'm much too busy. But you'd better go or Daddy will get cross.'

Louise descended slowly, overwhelmed by memories, and located Mark in the kitchen, pouring sherry into two glasses. He handed her one and raised his own in a silent toast.

'It seems a long time,' he said eventually.

'What does?'

'Since you were here.'

'It's nearly three months.'

'Really?' His eyes under the long, elegantly-shaped brows looked at her across the top of his glass. 'Louise—' he began uncertainly.

Her heart missed a beat. 'Yes?'

'I've got to talk to you. There's so much we have to say to each other.'

'I shouldn't have thought there was anything,' she said bitterly.

His reply came swiftly and was spoken with all his normal assurance. 'That's ridiculous. You must know we've *got* to talk—there's a lot of straightening out to be done.'

'Is there? I don't see any need for discussion. What could we possibly have to talk about?'

'For goodness sake don't be like that, Louise!' He snatched at her hand and held it so tightly that she winced with pain. 'You must know what I mean.'

'I was never very good at riddles and I'm not in the mood just now either, so let's leave things as they are, shall we?' Summoning all her resolution she tilted her chin and stared at him defiantly. 'I really think it would be better,' she finished firmly.

'You can think what you damn well like, but I'm not going to be dictated to when my mind's made up.' Mark dropped her hand and dragged her into his arms. 'What's the matter with you, Louise? You weren't like this after the ball.'

Swept by an emotion she couldn't control, her lips eagerly awaiting his kisses, Louise lifted her face and closed her eyes. But as Mark bent his head a clear cold voice spoke from the doorway.

'So! I come back after a most trying day and I find this! It is too much.' Anna's frosty blue gaze swept over them in furious condemnation. 'Louise, you will please to leave this house *at once*.'

CHAPTER ELEVEN

THEY MUST have looked terribly guilty, Louise thought afterwards. The two startled faces turned in Anna's direction made it only too clear she had not been expected back yet, and Louise's frantic attempt to release herself did nothing to help the situation.

Taking his time about it, Mark allowed his arms to fall to his sides. 'Was the car ready early?' he asked casually.

'Yes, it was! And no doubt you are sorry. You thought to end this—this pleasant little interlude before I returned, but I have caught you nicely. Louise—did you not hear what I said? I wish you to leave at once so that I may speak to Mark privately.'

'It may interest you to know,' Mark said icily, 'that Louise has been looking after Vicky since before lunch. If you hadn't hung up on Mrs Mayhew you would have discovered that she couldn't manage it.'

'And you thank her with kisses, is that so?'

'No, it is not so!' His control snapped abruptly. 'I'm sorry you arrived just then, Anna, but it might turn out for the best in the long run.'

Louise looked at him in astonishment, quite unable to grasp his meaning, and Anna seemed equally puzzled. As the Danish girl appeared to be unusually at a loss for words, Louise decided it was time she said something.

'You really mustn't upset yourself about what you've just seen,' she pointed out. 'It wasn't of the slightest importance and shouldn't affect you in any way. It will certainly never occur again.'

Mark looked at her sharply and said urgently, 'Louise—' but she cut in on him ruthlessly.

'I'm going now, Anna, and if I were you I'd forget all about this incident. I intend to.' And with her head held high she walked rather blindly into the hall.

She had just closed the front door when it was flung open again and Mark hurtled out, almost knocking her down.

'You can't go like this!' he exploded. 'I've still got a lot I want to say to you.'

'Do you want to cause Anna even more distress?' Louise demanded. 'I think you should go straight back and apologise to her— if you can bring yourself to do such a thing. I don't suppose apologising is much in your line as a rule.'

'Louise, for goodness sake, we've got to straighten this out. I'll drive you home and we'll talk on the way.' He made a grab at her arm but she avoided him.

'I don't want to be driven home, thank you.'
Somehow she kept her voice steady. 'I'd much
rather walk and give myself time to recover.
I—I don't know when I've felt so humiliated as
I did just now, when Anna appeared like that.
It was horrible!'

'It was certainly most unexpected,' Mark
agreed ruefully. And as Louise shrugged and
turned away, he called after her, 'I wish you'd
let me drive you. It's a lonely walk in the dusk.'

'I don't mind the loneliness.'

'I suppose anything's better than my company,' he suggested bitterly.

'You could put it like that.'

As soon as she was well away from the house
she unconsciously slackened her speed until
she was only sauntering. The evening air was
blessedly cool on her hot face and the quiet
misty marshes were infinitely soothing.
Gradually Anna's scornful voice stopped ringing in her ears and she began to regain a little of
her self-respect.

After all, it hadn't been her fault. She had
been as surprised as the housekeeper when
Mark took her in his arms, and the fact that she
had enjoyed it was beside the point. Or was it?
Perhaps, morally, she was just as guilty as
Anna believed.

For the first time Louise dared to put into
words her true feelings for Mark. She loved
him deeply, passionately—and hopelessly.

She had half known it for some while, of course—ever since he kissed her on the marshes, though it had been easy at the time to put that down to what he'd laughingly called midsummer madness. There was no madness about what she felt now. It was for real, and there was no hope at all of making herself believe anything else.

A willow sheltered her as she cried her heart out, and she left its overhanging branches in a much calmer frame of mind. Something would have to be done—some time—about this overwhelming and utterly hopeless love of hers, but she couldn't tear it out of her heart just yet. For a little while longer she must have the daily bitter-sweet experience of seeing Mark in the ward.

But after that evening at Creek House he only spoke to her when necessity demanded it and then with the utmost curtness. He was even at times abrupt with the other nurses, keeping his normal unfailing friendly attitude for his little patients alone.

'I wonder what's the matter with Dr Halliwell?' Sarah said one day. 'He looks grim enough to be on his way to an execution. Do you think his love life has gone awry?'

'Has he got one?' Louise asked listlessly.

'What do you mean? Has the Danish housekeeper left then?'

'Not as far as I know.'

'Living in the same village, I suppose you'd be sure to hear if she had. Maybe Mark has fallen out of love with her. He seems to go in somewhat for variety. What do you think?'

'I don't know anything about it.' Louise turned her back and went to investigate an outburst of crying from one of the cots.

It was in an effort to rouse herself from the depression which now seemed permanent that she decided to ring up Colin Mason. She hadn't seen him for some time and had no idea how his brother was. Enquiring after Robert would be a good excuse.

Colin sounded very cheerful on the phone but also in a tremendous hurry.

'I'm just going out, Louise, so I can't stop to talk. It's great to hear your voice again, though.'

'How's Rob?' she asked quickly before he could hang up.

'Doing fine, thank goodness, now he's finished his treatment. He's been at home for some time now and really seems to be a lot more optimistic about himself.'

'Oh, Colin, I *am* glad! He may not have a recurrence, you know. People don't always.'

'I certainly hope he'll be lucky,' Colin said soberly. His voice changed as he added, 'We must have a get-together some time, Louise, and catch up on the news. How about having a drink one evening when you come off duty and then I'll drive you home?'

'I'd enjoy that,' she told him, trying to infuse some warmth into the words.

'How about tomorrow then? That suit you?'

'Fine! I'll look out for you when I leave the hospital.'

At intervals during the following day Louise reminded herself sternly that she had, for once, something to look forward to that evening. It didn't make much difference to her outlook but at least she had tried.

Colin was waiting for her by the car park. Fair, too broad-shouldered for his height, he was the exact opposite of Mark and that was all to the good. Smiling radiantly, Louise advanced to meet him, and was at once conscious of that same extra-special cheerfulness she had noticed on the phone.

'The car's over here.' He tucked his arm in hers and steered her in the right direction. 'I've got a surprise for you, love,' he added in a slightly awkward tone.

'New car?'

'Oh no—nothing like that.' He laughed self-consciously. 'Come on and in a few seconds all will be revealed.'

Puzzled, Louise allowed him to speed up their rate of progress. They squeezed between a Mini and a Metro, and came suddenly upon his slightly shabby blue car.

'There you are!' Colin waved his arm with a conjuror-like gesture.

Celia Browning sat in the front seat.

Louise came to an involuntary halt, feeling ridiculously taken aback. Exactly what it all meant she didn't at present understand, but it was plain enough that the cheering-up evening she had imagined she was to have with Colin was to become a threesome.

'Surprise, surprise!' she said gaily as she got into the back seat. 'How's life been treating you, Celia? I haven't seen you for ages.'

'It's been treating me very well.' The small dark girl turned round with a smile. 'It was the luckiest thing I ever did, coming to Marchester—and meeting Colin.' She glanced at him as he started the engine. 'I suppose you haven't told her yet?'

'I thought you'd like to do it.'

And so it all came pouring out. They had fallen in love when he came to visit his brother in hospital, and now they were engaged and going to be married at Christmas.

'And if you hadn't changed wards with me,' Celia finished, 'none of it would have happened because I wouldn't even have known Colin existed. It's all your doing, Louise.'

And if she hadn't agreed to the change, she wouldn't have been brought into such close contact with Mark. The thought leapt unbidden into her mind but Louise thrust it away defensively. It didn't do to go through life thinking on those lines. Things happened, or didn't happen, and it was best to accept that there might be some sort of pattern to it.

'It's ridiculous to say that.' She forced a laugh. 'You'd probably have been drawn to each other somehow or other.'

'I'd like to think so,' Colin said fondly.

By the end of the evening Louise was finding their absorption in each other rather too much to bear. They did their best not to exclude her from their happiness, but unfortunately she was aware all the time that they were doing it. Or was she being super-sensitive? Whatever the true state of affairs, Louise was glad when she could put an end to it without giving offence.

'If I don't see you again before Christmas,' she said lightly when she had been delivered to Deenham Station and was about to mount her bicycle, 'I hope you have an absolutely super wedding.'

'You must come to it, of course,' Celia told her eagerly. 'It's to be in Marchester because my mother is a widow and I haven't many relations. Colin has lots around here so it would be better to marry locally.'

'I'll certainly come if I can, but I don't know where I shall be at Christmas. I'm only temporary at Marchester, you know, the same as you're supposed to be. We were only sent there for the holiday period and that's over now.'

'I think we're still needed. As a matter of fact, I'm going to leave the agency and ask if I can go on the staff. Why don't you do that too if you're enjoying living at home again?'

'Oh no, I like agency work,' Louise said fervently.

Her next remark startled even herself. It seemed to come into her head and out of her mouth without actually being thought first, but as soon as it was said she realised what a good idea it was.

'Personally, I think I've been at Marchester long enough and I'm going to ring up Mrs Acland and ask her if I can go back to private nursing. I'm sure she could find me an interesting job.'

Celia made no comment and Louise sensed disapproval. Not that it mattered. What she had just said was quite clearly her best course of action and she couldn't imagine why it had taken her so long to think of it.

She had fought hard against falling in love with Mark and she had lost the battle. It might be cowardly to run away and it would hurt terribly. But it wouldn't hurt as much as staying.

'You'll have to give proper notice, dear,' Mrs Acland said when she phoned the next day. 'You can't just walk out.'

'A whole month?' Louise asked in dismay.

'Not as long as that, since you're only temporary. You could probably get away with a week's notice, but I think a fortnight would be more considerate. I take it you'd like your next job to be a private case?'

'Yes, I think so, though I've enjoyed the hospital experience and also brought myself up to date on one or two things. I don't necessarily want to go abroad again—anywhere in this country will do.' So long as it's not in this area, she added silently as she replaced the receiver.

She should have been feeling thankful she had burnt her boats, but instead she was obliged to battle against steadily growing unhappiness. Added to the pain in her heart there was the regret that she would be leaving Anderson ward, where she had so much enjoyed nursing.

The Senior Nursing Officer to whom she gave her notice was philosophical, though not particularly pleased. No doubt, Louise thought regretfully, she considered all agency nurses thoroughly undependable. Liz received the news of her impending departure quietly, making very little comment beyond a rather formal expression of regret.

'Have you got another job to go to?' she asked.

'I shan't get fixed up with one until I leave

here. People who want private nurses usually send in an urgent request for them, so I shall probably have a few days holiday before starting something new—unless, of course, I'm lucky and get offered another job as soon as I'm free.'

At first the days passed slowly, but towards the end they began to accelerate to a terrifying degree and suddenly it was the last morning for cycling to the station. Louise started early and rode more slowly than usual. Looking back over her daily rides she remembered times when she had hated them—usually because of bad weather or because she had been late and had to rush—but mostly they had been enjoyable. She would miss them when she left home again.

In the ward she had said very little about leaving, but Liz remembered it was her last day and called her into the office to say goodbye before she went off to catch her evening train.

'I hope you get the sort of job you want,' she said with a friendly smile. 'We shall miss you, of course, but at least the holidays are all over now.' Her face changed as she looked over Louise's shoulder at someone who had appeared in the doorway. 'Can I help you, Mark?'

He ignored the question. In fact, he was not looking at Sister at all but at the back of

Louise's head. Slowly, unwillingly, she turned to face him.

'I didn't know you were leaving,' he said harshly.

'I was only temporary,' she reminded him, 'and I've already been here longer than I expected.'

'You're going back to private nursing?'

'Yes.'

'No doubt you'll prefer that.'

There seemed to be no reply needed except a shrug. With a smile for Liz, Louise slipped past him and almost ran to the locker room. Fortunately it was empty and it did not matter that she could no longer control her emotions. Fighting against tears and not being very successful, she collected her few belongings and left the hospital.

'Has Mrs Acland rung up?' she asked her mother as soon as she reached home.

Marion shook her head. 'You're in an awful hurry to get away,' she complained. 'I thought you were enjoying living at home again?'

'Oh yes, of course I was.' Louise hastened to reassure her. 'But it'll soon be winter and travelling to Marchester every day wouldn't be much fun in really bad weather. Besides, I guess I'm one of those people who like lots of variety.'

Her mother looked at her dubiously and

made no further comment, but Louise had an
uneasy feeling that there was a great deal she
would have liked to say.

After the first two days of waiting for the
summons from the agency, it became difficult
to fill in the time. Somehow the marshes had
lost their charm and she no longer walked in
that direction. Most of the time she stayed
close to the house and garden, anxious not to
miss a phone call, but occasionally she was
obliged to go into the village to make odd
purchases at the shop.

She was returning from one of these brief
expeditions when she saw an ancient bicycle
being ridden slowly along the road which led to
Creek House. No one else locally except
William Taunton had such an outdated model
and she could only assume that he must be
going to do some gardening.

He was due at Holly Lodge the following
afternoon and it wasn't difficult for Louise to
lead the conversation in the direction which
she wanted it to follow.

'I expect you're kept pretty busy, William,
even though the summer is over?'

'Lord bless you, yes. The grass is still growing and wants cutting regular.' He straightened his back and scratched beneath the cap
which covered his thick, iron-grey hair. His
face was ruddy and healthy-looking and it was
hard to believe that he had ever fainted in the

train because of the heat. 'I took on a new job last week, though I couldn't rightly spare the time for it.'

'Where was that?' Louise asked innocently.

'At Creek House. Dr Halliwell asked me if I'd do a bit of work for him and I couldn't refuse after he'd saved our Kathy's life when she was so ill. Proper mess his garden is and no mistake,' he added ruefully. 'Rum set-up altogether if you ask me.'

'Did you—did you see the little girl?'

'Oh yes. I was there afore she went off to school. Nice little thing but a bit peaky-looking.' William carefully hoed round one of the rose bushes and Louise, sensing that he had something further to comment on, kept silent.

''Tisn't good for a child to listen to people quarrelling,' he volunteered at last. 'That foreign woman, she can't half let fly when she's in a temper. You should have heard her the other day—something shocking it was.'

'It couldn't have been very nice for Vicky,' Louise agreed. 'I suppose she was having a row with the doctor?'

'Musta been, though he was speaking quiet-like and I couldn't hear nothing from him at all.'

Louise could imagine it. Anna in a furious mood, with her blue eyes flashing, and Mark growing steadily more icy and curt, yet with every verbal thrust calculated to give the maximum amount of pain.

But why should he want to hurt Anna?

No doubt their relationship was frequently stormy, she reminded herself as she left William to get on with his work. Very likely the cause of the quarrel was something quite trivial which one or the other of them had built up into a tremendous issue which could only be settled by a slanging match.

Nevertheless, her mind continued to worry at the matter as she went indoors, and it was only the ringing of the telephone which enabled her to shelve it for the time being.

In a doctor's house the phone was always ringing and she was not very hopeful as she lifted the receiver. But this time it really was Mrs Acland with a job for her.

'It's in Surrey, dear, so I suppose you'll have to come up to London first. A case of hypostatic pneumonia—an elderly man living with his married daughter. He'll need a lot of care and I'm sending them a night nurse as well. Will you get there as early as possible in the morning, please?'

Louise glanced at her watch. 'I could make it today if you like.'

'There's no need. The night nurse is prepared to carry on till you turn up and I've arranged it all now. I wasn't sure how long the journey would take you. She's a nice girl—

very obliging—and I told her you lived some distance from London and couldn't get there at the drop of a hat.'

She went rattling on, giving Louise the name and address and other details, and then hung up. Replacing her own receiver slowly, Louise stood lost in thought. So it had come—the summons she had been longing for, the chance to get away from Barkington and a hopeless love, and make a fresh start.

Then why didn't she feel more cheerful?

After breaking the news to her mother, she began packing, determined to leave as early as possible in the morning. This job probably wouldn't be a long one, she reasoned, but she ought to take as much as she could manage with her in case she got sent straight to another one.

She had filled her big case and put a few things into her overnight bag when she heard the phone ringing again. Her mother was downstairs so she made no attempt to answer it. After all, it was very unlikely to be for her.

But she couldn't have been more wrong.

'Louise!' Marion's voice came floating up the stairs. 'You're wanted on the phone, dear.'

'Who is it?'

'I don't know. All I can tell you is that it was a man's voice and he sounded in a desperate hurry, so I didn't stop to ask his name. You'd better come quickly.'

Perhaps it was Colin. Not particularly interested but nevertheless hurrying as requested, Louise went down to the hall. She said 'Hello' and then very nearly dropped the receiver.

'You must come at once!' It was Mark's voice and he sounded frantic. 'You've got to help me, Louise! Vicky's disappeared and I've reason to believe she may have gone out on to the marshes.'

CHAPTER TWELVE

NEVER HAD the road to Creek House seemed so long. Louise pedalled furiously, driven by the desperation in Mark's appeal to her and her own terrible fears. The wind caused by her speed rushed past her ears but there was another sound as well—the rippling and gurgling of water as all the little creeks came to life.

The tide was coming in.

He was standing on the bank when she got there, shading his eyes as he scanned the vast expanse of green and brown. Even at a time like that his greeting was typical.

'I thought you'd never come.'

'I hurried as much as I could. What's happened, Mark, and why do you think Vicky's gone off across the marshes?'

'Two reasons. I came home to find the house empty—'

'Anna?'

'She's gone. Packed up and departed, leaving a note behind her. *And* leaving Vicky alone. I could half kill her for that,' he added savagely.

Louise didn't ask why Anna had vanished.

Her heart had given a great leap of something very like exultation, and then the deadly seriousness of the situation took hold of her again.

'There was a terrible scene this morning,' Mark went on, 'Vicky was making an awful fuss because Anna had promised to take her to the beach as soon as she could walk that far, and she hadn't kept her promise. I had to leave for Marchester in the middle of it, so I don't know exactly what happened eventually, but I'm quite convinced that's where Vicky is. If she'd wandered off to the village someone would have seen her.'

It was logical reasoning, Louise had to admit that, 'Did she take her red anorak?' she asked briskly.

'It's missing. I checked that at once, so I expect she's wearing it. If only we had some binoculars—'

'I brought my father's.' She dragged them out of her bicycle bag. 'It shouldn't be too difficult to pick her up, Mark.' Knowing that he would want to look for himself, she handed the glasses to him.

He snatched them from her and raked the marshes with his eyes for a few seconds in silence. Louise waited as patiently as she could and tried not to think about the inexorable approach of the sea. Mark must know as well as she did that the tide was coming in and sooner or later one of them would have to mention it.

Suddenly he gave an exclamation. 'There's a tiny spot of red in the far distance. It's Vicky for sure! Come on, Louise—you'll be able to show me the best way to get to her.'

'There's only one way—along the creek bank.' It was the route he had taken the evening they met on the beach but she did not remind him. 'The creeks will all be filling up,' she added in a worried tone. 'I'm afraid that, by the time we get to the breaks in the bank, they may be too wide to jump.'

'We've got to jump them, or at least *I* have,' he told her impatiently.

She followed him uneasily and at first it was quite simple. On their left the brown water of the main creek flowed steadily inland but the bank was well above it and the criss-cross pattern of the little creeks on the other side of them presented no danger.

Then they came to the first break, a fairly narrow one which they both crossed without difficulty, pausing immediately afterwards to use the glasses again.

'I can't see her.' Mark said anxiously.

'She's so little. If she was sitting down, she could easily be hidden by one of those huge clumps of marsh grass.'

He caught her hand and held it tightly for a moment. 'You're a great comfort, Louise.

When Vicky disappeared you were the first person I thought of.'

'I—I'm so glad I was there and able to come,' she said shakily. If it had happened tomorrow instead of today, she wouldn't even have known about it.

They went on again but were brought to a halt by a wide gap through which the water was racing to join the creek. Louise looked at it in horror. It was even worse than she had expected and she knew she couldn't possibly hope to get across.

'We'll have to go back and round by the other route. It's too late to reach the beach this way.' She spoke without looking at him so he shouldn't see the panic in her eyes.

'What other route?' he demanded. 'You said this was the only way.'

'It's the only way on foot, but there's a track used by cars which also leads to the beach further along.' Again, just for a brief moment, her thoughts flew to the last time she had been down there.

'How far is it?'

'I'm afraid it's quite a long way from here but if we hurry—'

'No!' His jaw was set and his face unyielding. 'I'm not going to waste all that time when I know I can get over these little creeks somehow and reach Vicky much more quickly. She'll be terrified, poor little scrap, if she sees the sea getting nearer and nearer. She may even try to come back this way and who knows what might happen then.' His voice shook.

Louise knew he was right. Speed was of the utmost importance.

'You'll have to go on without me,' she said, 'and you must do it immediately too, or you won't have a hope. As it is, you'll probably get soaked.'

'Who cares about that if Vicky is safe?' Mark thrust his hand into his pocket. 'Take my car, Louise, and drive round by the track. We'll meet you on the beach.' He handed her the keys and without another word leapt across the gap.

Louise watched despairingly as his feet slipped on the muddy bank and he began to slide back into the water. But a quick scramble saved him and he was off again, half running along the path.

If only she could have gone with him and shared the danger, but she would merely have been a hindrance. He would travel faster and more safely alone. Wrenching her gaze from his hurrying figure, she resolutely set herself to carry out her instructions as quickly as possible.

At any other time the thought of driving his precious car would have terrified her, and certainly Mark would never have suggested it. But now she was cool and resolute as she

examined the unfamiliar controls and started
the engine. It sprang powerfully to life and
leapt ahead as she let in the clutch, so that she
nearly scraped the gatepost as she left Creek
House.

The road to the village, which had seemed
so long only a short time ago, vanished in a few
minutes. Concentrating totally on what she
was doing, not allowing herself to think of
what might be happening to Mark or Vicky,
Louise drove through the village and came to
where the rough track turned off across the
marshes.

No one else was using it on that autumn
afternoon and she bumped along as fast as she
dared. She was frightened again now as her
thoughts inevitably flew to the man and the
child, both of them in such dreadful danger.
She had no doubt that Mark confidently believed he would get to the beach in safety, but
he didn't realise fully how quickly the creeks
could fill—or the evil strength of the horrible,
clutching mud. If he once allowed it to get
hold of him he wouldn't be able to free himself.

There was still plenty of beach at this end,
though tiny channels from the sea were flowing
up it. Louise began to run, her eyes seeking
desperately for that small patch of bright red.
But there was a point of slightly higher land
between her and the far end and she could see

nothing except sea and mud and tussocks of grass.

She was gasping for breath as she came at last to the obstruction which blocked her view. It was only two or three metres above the beach but the mud made it slippery and she scrambled round it instead of going straight over, regardless of wet feet. As soon as she reached the other side she stopped and stared ahead, and suddenly all the anxiety and tension of the last half-hour caught up with her and she burst into tears.

Mark was coming towards her, holding his little daughter by the hand.

Louise's legs were trembling so much that she was obliged to sit down, but she had herself under control by the time they arrived and was able to stand up and greet them with a smile.

Vicky looked pale and tired, and there were traces of tears, but she had recovered sufficiently to comment gleefully on Mark's appearance.

'Hasn't Daddy got himself into a mess! Just look at his trousers.'

Louise had already noticed them. He was mud to the waist and his dark hospital suit was quite ruined, but he, too, was smiling.

'It was a near thing when I jumped the last creek,' he said, 'but I just made it. I think Vicky was quite pleased to see me, weren't you, love?'

Louise closed her eyes for a moment as she imagined the situation had he not just made it, and then she pulled herself together in time to laugh outright at Vicky's reply.

'I was getting just a little bit lonely, and I don't think I like the sea being so big. Couldn't we find a smaller one somewhere and live near that?'

'We'll have to see what can be done,' Mark told her. His eyes were on Louise as he added quietly, 'Creek House hasn't been quite the peaceful retreat I expected.'

Was he saying that because of the row with Anna? Or could it be due to the fright which Vicky had given him?

Some time she might find out the answers to those two questions but, in the meantime, she must concentrate on Vicky, getting her back home and into a hot bath and then bed. The early October dusk was already creeping mistily across the marshes and its damp breath was chilling all three of them. Eventually Mark picked up Vicky and carried her, and so they came to the waiting car.

'I hope it's okay, Louise,' he said with a grin. 'No scraped wings or dented bumpers?'

'Of course not! I was very careful.'

They drove back to Creek House at a far greater speed than hers had been, even though she had believed herself to be hurrying. Automatically, without being asked, she went up-

stairs with the little girl, bathed her quickly
and got her to bed, exhausted by her ordeal
and already almost asleep.

'The bathroom's all yours!' she called out to
Mark, and soon he was splashing in hot water,
removing all traces of the mud.

When he came downstairs he was wearing
sports trousers and a thick navy sweater. His
hair, wet and waving slightly, was on end and
he looked younger than she had ever seen him.
There was hot coffee waiting for him in the
percolator but first he insisted on something
stronger.

'Whisky's what we need,' he said firmly. 'I
never want to go through such an experience
again as long as I live.'

'The marshes can be terrifying.'

'I'll say!' For a moment she saw a reflection
in his eyes of what he had been through. 'Shall
I tell you something, Louise? I never understood how much Vicky meant to me until she
got herself into that awful situation. If it hadn't
ended up all right I—I don't know what I
would have done.'

'Oh, Mark!' Swept by emotion, she went
over to him and put her hand on his arm.
'Don't think about it—just be thankful it's
made you see Vicky differently. She's such a
dear little girl and she shouldn't have to get all
her affection from—from someone like
Anna.'

She had never meant to mention the name. She had made up her mind that Mark must be the one to introduce Anna into the conversation and perhaps explain what had happened. But now it was done and she waited with a fast-beating heart to see what his reaction would be.

'Until today,' Mark said tautly, 'Anna was very good to Vicky. I could trust her absolutely.'

'Until today?'

'Come and sit down, and I'll tell you about it.' He drew her towards a small, shabby sofa which stood against the wall in the kitchen.

There was just room for two and Louise was very conscious of his nearness, of the hard feel of his shoulder against hers and the spicy smell of some sort of masculine talc. He was still holding her hand and if what he was saying hadn't been so desperately important she would have found it hard to take it all in.

'Anna and I have quarrelled quite a lot lately,' Mark explained. 'It was partly my fault—I know I was uptight and bad-tempered, but she used to take my moods in her stride and then, suddenly, she stopped doing so. I think it was partly that she didn't much care for living in this isolated spot but there was more to it than that.'

He came to a halt. Louise waited for a moment and then prodded gently.

'That doesn't account for her going off so abruptly, and even leaving Vicky.'

'Last night things came to a head. She accused me of letting her think I would marry her one day. She seemed to imagine that because she was my housekeeper and young and attractive, marriage was the natural thing. I told her I didn't love her, that I'd never loved her, and she was furious. It—it was a disgusting scene.' He tightened his grip on Louise's hand.

'I can understand that she was disappointed. And I'm a bit puzzled as to why she gave up hope. She's always seemed a very determined person and I would have expected her to keep on trying.'

'There would have been no point in that at all. I told her I was in love with you,' Mark said simply.

Louise turned her head slowly and looked at him. She said, 'You what?' in a very small voice, and then suddenly she was as angry as Anna must have been.

'So you made use of a lie to get out of a difficult situation which was entirely your own fault? You had absolutely no right to involve me in it.' She snatched her hand away and leapt to her feet. 'It was a filthy thing to do,' she stormed at him, 'but I suppose it was on a par with the rest of your behaviour—kissing people in lay-bys and importing glamorous so-called housekeepers into your home and—

and—' She broke off as suddenly as she had begun.

'Shut up!' Mark, too, was on his feet and he took hold of her by the shoulders and shook her. 'What the hell makes you think I told a lie about loving you? It was the truth, do you hear me? I've loved you for weeks, but I knew you loathed and despised me so there didn't seem much sense in telling you.'

He stopped shouting abruptly and smoothed her tawny hair back from her forehead with a gentle hand. 'Would there have been any sense in it, Louise? Please tell me, I have to know where I stand.'

He was looking deep into her eyes and her answer must have been plainly written there, for he scarcely waited for her stammered reply before folding his arms about her and gathering her to him as though he never meant to let her go again.

They were back on the little sofa and she was lying across his lap when Louise again became conscious of her surroundings. His kisses were still sweet on her lips and her whole body was alive and responsive. Dreamily she nestled her head into the curve of his shoulder and felt his cheek against her hair, and it seemed to her that life could never offer a greater bliss.

'Is it really true?' she asked after a while.

'Of course it's true.' He kissed her passionately, his mouth hard against hers. 'When can we get married? Please let it be soon.'

For no reason at all Louise's mind flew to the connecting door between his room and Anna's. *Had* they been lovers? A small part of her longed to know the answer, but the more sensible and mature side knew that it would be better to remain in ignorance. The past was past and Mark was hers now.

Perhaps he had half-read her thoughts for he said suddenly, 'I've never loved anyone since my wife betrayed me. You believe that, don't you?'

'I believe it.'

'Then let's get married as quickly as possible. How about next week?'

Louise laughed happily. 'I couldn't be ready as soon as that. You'll have to find a new housekeeper for a little while—somebody middle-aged, please, but as soon as I finish my new job we'll get down to making plans.'

'What new job?' He was outraged.

As gently as possible she explained that she was leaving in the morning and was not surprised when he exploded with wrath.

'You can't possibly go away and leave me when I've only just found you. Ring up that damn agency and tell them you've changed your mind—and they needn't send you any more jobs either, because you're quitting.'

'I'll tell them that last bit,' Louise agreed,

'but I must do the job they've just sent me. I couldn't possibly let them down, Mark, dear. You must see that, surely?'

'I don't see anything of the sort,' he said mutinously, and then his face softened. 'Okay, love. I suppose you wouldn't be much of a nurse if you did back out now. How long are you likely to be away?'

'Perhaps only a week, and I shall miss you just as much as you seem to think you're going to miss me. We can talk on the phone every evening—'

'I can't kiss you over the phone.'

'We'll make up for that when I get back.' And as his arms enfolded her again she added softly, 'We'll have all the rest of our lives to make up for it.'

All the time in the world in which to remove the last traces of his bitterness and teach him how to be happy.

Doctor Nurse Romances

Mills & Boon

4 Doctor Nurse Romances
FREE

Coping with the daily tragedies and ordeals of a busy hospital, and sharing the satisfaction of a difficult job well done, people find themselves unexpectedly drawn together. Mills & Boon Doctor Nurse Romances capture perfectly the excitement, the intrigue and the emotions of modern medicine, that so often lead to overwhelming and blissful love. By becoming a regular reader of Mills & Boon Doctor Nurse Romances you can enjoy EIGHT superb new titles every two months plus a whole range of special benefits: your very own personal membership card, a free newsletter packed with recipes, competitions, bargain book offers, plus big cash savings.

**AND an Introductory FREE GIFT for YOU.
Turn over the page for details.**

**Fill in and send this coupon back today
and we'll send you
4 Introductory
Doctor Nurse Romances yours to keep**

FREE

At the same time we will reserve a
subscription to Mills & Boon
Doctor Nurse Romances for you. Every
two months you will receive the latest
8 new titles, delivered direct to your door.
You don't pay extra for delivery. Postage and
packing is always completely Free.
There is no obligation or commitment –
you receive books only for
as long as you want to.

It's easy! Fill in the coupon below and return it to
**MILLS & BOON READER SERVICE, FREEPOST, P.O. BOX 236,
CROYDON, SURREY CR9 9EL.**

**Please note: READERS IN SOUTH AFRICA write to
Mills & Boon Ltd., Postbag X3010,
Randburg 2125, S. Africa.**

- - - - - - - - - - - - - - - - - -

FREE BOOKS CERTIFICATE

**To: Mills & Boon Reader Service, FREEPOST, P.O. Box 236,
Croydon, Surrey CR9 9EL.**

Please send me, free and without obligation, four Dr Nurse Romances, and reserve a
Reader Service Subscription for me. If I decide to subscribe I shall receive, following my free
parcel of books, eight new Dr Nurse Romances every two months for £8.00, post and
packing free. If I decide not to subscribe, I shall write to you within 10 days. The free books
are mine to keep in any case. I understand that I may cancel my subscription at any time
simply by writing to you. I am over 18 years of age.
Please write in BLOCK CAPITALS.

Name _____

Address _____

_____

_____ Postcode _____

SEND NO MONEY — TAKE NO RISKS

EP